Pentecostal Churches in Kerala
and
Indigenous Leadership

Pentecostal Churches in Kerala
and
Indigenous Leadership

Ipe Kochupallikunnel

ISPCK
Impacting Communities since 1710

2011

Pentecostal Churches in Kerala and Indigenous Leadership – Published by Rev. Dr. Ashish Amos of the Indian Society for Promoting Christian Knowledge (ISPCK), Post Box 1585, 1654, Madarsa Road, Kashmere Gate, Delhi-110006.

ISBN : 978-81-8465-147-8

Laser typeset and cover design by **ISPCK,** Post Box 1585, 1654, Madarsa Road, Kashmere Gate, Delhi-110006.
Tel: 23866323, 23866323
e-mail: ashish@ispck.org.in • ella@ispck.org.in
website: www.ispck.org.in

Contents

CHAPTER I

Background of the Origin of the Pentecostal Churches in Kerala

CHAPTER II

Origin of Pentecostal Churches and the Emergence of Indigenous Leadership

CHAPTER III

Progress of the Church Under Indigenous Leadership

CHAPTER IV

Impact of Indigenous Leadership

Acknowlegements

As a member of an 'Independent Pentecostal Church' in Kerala, 'Indigenous leadership among the Pentecostals' is a topic of my personal interest. Local church should be progressed under the guidance of the Holy Spirit, as in the days of Apostles, enjoying the freedom it deserves.

I thank almighty God for his abundant grace and providence showered upon me to complete the M.Th programme and especially to accomplish this research work. There are many to whom I have to express my profound gratitude and deep indebtedness, but I regret that it is not possible to mention all of them by name.

First of all, I express my gratitude to Rev.Fr.Dr.M.O.John who gave me valuable guidance, suggestions and timely corrections which enabled me to complete the thesis in time. It is my great pleasure to extend my gratitude to Rev.Dr.T.G.Koshy, The Founded President of Faith Theological Seminary, Manakala, Adoor, for his loving concern, encouragement and financial support for my theological studies.

I thank the Pentecostal leaders who gave needed information to furnish this work. I also acknowledge my friends, relatives and church-members for their whole-hearted prayers and co-operation. Besides I thank the Librarians of Mar Thoma Theological Seminary – Kottayam, Orthodox Theological Seminary – Kottayam, St.Thomas Apostolic Seminary (Vadavathoor)-Kottayam, Thomas Mar Athanasius Orientation Centre (Manganam) – Faith Theological Seminary

– Adoor, Bethel Bible College – Punalur, and Kerala United Theological Seminary (Kannammoola) – Trivandrum for their kind help.

I record my gratitude to the Manager, Deepam Graphics, Nagampadam, Kottayam and especially to Mr.Manoj T.S. who typed the thesis neatly.

– Rev.Ipe Kochupallikunnel. M.Th

Faith Theological Seminary
Manakala

Introduction

Marked with the outpouring of the Holy Spirit modern Pentecostal Movement began in the Twentieth century. From its very beginning missionaries came to India from United States of America and other European countries. With the co-operation of natives they could establish many churches and it progressed by the financial assistance and administrative control of the missionaries. Since there were no able native leadership for the Pentecostal movement in Kerala, it was possible for the missionaries to control the work. But when the natives who had potential leadership joined with the Pentecostal movement in 1920's and attempted to bring the church under the natives, tension arose between the natives and the missionaries. Thus the struggle between natives and missionaries resulted in division and indigenous leadership emerged among the Pentecostals at the beginning of 1930.

PURPOSE

The present paper is an attempt to investigate the development of native leadership among the Pentecostals in Kerala. The study highlight the struggles for indigenous leadership among the Pentecostals and to bring out the ways and means adopted to achieve the same. It aims to understand the emphasis given by the native leadership for the independence of the Pentecostal churches from foreign domination and the results achieved by it. It also tries to understand the indigenous principles applied to the development of Pentecostal churches and challenges the Pentecostal leadership to stand by their own for the progress of the church.

SCOPE

As the title implies, this study is geographically confined to the state of Kerala. We do not deal every aspect of the history of Pentecostal churches but concentrate on the struggle for indigenous leadership and its implication in the life and mission of the Pentecostal churches. Though there are many Pentecostal churches in progress under native leadership, we limit our study with major Pentecostal churches namely, Indian Pentecostal Church of God, Assemblies of God, Church of God (Full Gospel) in India, and Sharon Fellowship Church. Socio-religious and political condition of Kerala serve as the background for this study.

METHOD

The present study is done in the historical perspective, highlighting the important issues related to the indigenous leadership. Historical analysis is made upon the available sources such as old records, biographies, books, and articles published in journals.

SOURCES

Library sources, such as books and articles written both in English and Malayalam on the Pentecostal movement, are mainly used for this study. Needed information is collected from the primary and secondary sources. Primary sources include published books, autobiographies and articles from journals like 'Pentecostu Kahalam', 'Suvisesha Prabhashakan', 'Pentecostal Evangel', 'Zion Kahalam',etc.- written by pioneers and other Pentecostal leaders. Booklets and brochures of the movement, letters of correspondence, minutes and reports of the church are also used to get primary information. Secondary sources used for this study include published books, articles from various journals like 'Good news', 'Malabar Gospel Messenger', 'Assemblies of God Messenger', 'Jeevadhara', etc., and previous research papers. Some information been have collected through personal interviews with Pentecostal leaders.

DEFINITION OF KEY TERMS

The word 'indigenous' is commonly used among the Christian circles in two senses. In one sense the word meant for the younger churches and their freedom to develop on their own lines without rigid control from the West. This principle was fully accepted in the non-Roman, Christian world from about 1890.[1] The word 'indigenous' is used for the church which progress independent from foreign mission body.

The term 'Pentecostal' has been derived from the Greek word 'pentekoste' which literally means "fifty". It is the Greek name for the Jewish festival known as the "feast of weeks" in the Old Testament, which celebrates the fiftieth day after Passover. The Holy Spirit descended upon the disciples on the day of Pentecost, as Jesus promised.[2] Christians who believe in the possibilities of receiving the same experience of baptism in the Holy Spirit as in the days of apostles, on the day of Pentecost are called "Pentecostals".[3] One of the features of the Pentecostals is the doctrine of 'baptism' in the 'Holy Spirit' with the evidence of 'speaking in tongues'.[4]

CONTENT

The first chapter begins with, brief description on the socio-religious and political condition of Kerala and attempts for Indian leadership among the Thomas Christians to understand the context in which the Pentecostals' struggle for native leadership. It also gives an account of revivals in Kerala which

---

[1] Stephen Neill "Indegenization" Stephen Neill, *et.al.* (eds.), *Concise Dictionary of the Christian World Mission* (London: Luttworth Press, 1970), p.275.

[2] Acts of the Apostles 1:8 and 2:1-4.

[3] Stanley M.Burgess and Gray B.McGee, (eds.), *Dictionary of Pentecostal and Charismatic Movements*, rev.ed. (Michigan: Zonderva Publishing House, 1990), p.688.

[4] Walter J.Hollenweger, "After Twenty years Research on Pentecostalism", *International Review of Mission*, 75/297 (January, 1986), p.6.

helped to prepare the ground for the advent and rapid spread of Pentecostal churches.

The second chapter is dealt with the beginning of Modern Pentecostal Movement through the revivals in Topeka, Kansas to Azusa Street in United States of America, and the formation of Pentecostal congregations in Kerala by the work of early Pentecostal missionaries who experienced the blessings of Azusa Street revival. They describe the struggle for native leadership and the emergence of it by the beginning of 1930.

The Third Chapter gives the brief description of developments in major Pentecostal churches and their progress. While **Indian Pentecostal Church of God** and Sharon Fellowship Church progress under native leadership, **Assemblies of God** too transferred the responsibilities from missionaries to the natives. But Church of God (Full Gospel) in India is governed by the natives, who are appointed by the General Overseer in Cleveland, Tennessee.

Final Chapter deals with the impact of indigenous leadership upon the major Pentecostal churches in its progress, unity, identity, self-support and self-propagation, theological education and missionary work. It also challenges the native leadership to progress in indigenous principle, in every respect.

List of Abbreviations

AG	:	Assemblies of God.
BMS	:	Baptist Missionary Society.
CEM	:	Christian Evangelical Movement.
CGI	:	Church of God [Full Gospel] in India.
CLS	:	Christian Literature Society.
CMS	:	Church Missionary Society.
FTS	:	Faith Theological Seminary.
HMC	:	Home Missionary Council.
ICPF	:	Inter Collegiate Prayer Fellowship.
IPC	:	Indian Pentecostal Church of God.
KPF	:	Kerala Pentecostal Fellowship.
LMS	:	London Missionary Society.
NIV	:	New International Version.
PPAI	:	Pentecostal Press Association of India.
PSTS	:	Pentecostal Society for Theological Studies.
SIAG	:	South India Assemblies of God.
SPCK	:	Society for Promoting Christian Knowledge.
TLC	:	Theological Literature Committee.
USA	:	United States of America.

CHAPTER I

Background of the Origin of the Pentecostal Churches in Kerala

1.1. Political and Socio-Religious Background

Kerala, an integral part of the Indian sub-continent, is bounded by the Western Ghats on the East and the Arabian Sea on the West. Its unique geographical position and peculiar physical features have invested Kerala with a distinct individuality.[1] In the middle ages, Kerala was divided into many kingdoms and principalities engaged in endless wars. But in the beginning of the 18th century three major kingdoms of Calicut in North Kerala, Cochin in Central Kerala and Travancore in the South established powerful and permanent kingdoms of their own. Travancore was one of the earliest among the princely states to cultivate friendship with the English East India Company. The Mysorean invasion was a blessing in disguise for the English to increase their power in Kerala. The local rulers like the Zamorin sought their help in throwing off the Mysorean yoke. The English troops actively helped the Zamorin and the local chieftains in their fight against the Mysore rulers. The rulers of Cochin and Malabar agreed to pay an annual tribute to the English as English assured to protect them from foreign aggression. Thus British supremacy was firmly established all over Kerala following the Mysorean

---

[1] A.Sreedhara Menon, *A Survey of Kerala History* (Kottayam: Sahitya Pravartaka Co-operative Society Ltd., 1970), p.1.

invasion.[2] The British appointed residents to these states to interfere in the internal administration and the British domination was felt in all branches of administration. This state of affairs continued till India's independence. However the unified Kerala state came into existence only by November 1956, on the linguistic basis.

The establishment of British rule in India and economic policies pursued by the East India Company had the unfortunate consequence of a tremendous drain on India's resources.[3] Frequent famines were the order of the day. Native industries crippled and virtually obliterated as a result of the deliberate policy of exploitation. The western education imparted to them gave a new hope of emancipation and enlightenment. The Indian national movement was the outcome of several factors that influenced the minds of the people during the second half of the 19th century. Indians who went abroad for higher studies were inspired by the French revolution, Italian unification and American war of independence.[4] They carried those ideas to India and developed a national spirit among people. With the assumption of the leadership of the Indian National Congress by Mahatma Gandhi in 1920 began a new era in the history of the national movement in Malabar as well. The non-co-operation and civil-disobedience movements made considerable headway in Malabar.

Towards the close of the nineteenth century, the educated middle class in Travancore were greatly dissatisfied due to the exclusion of the educated natives from the higher grades of public service. In protest against this policy of the government, a mass petition, signed by more than ten thousand

---

[2] *Ibid.,* pp.313, 315.

[3] C.V.Cherian, *Indian History* Vol.II (Trivandrum: Kerala University Central Co-operative Stores Limited, 1991), p.158.

[4] M.Girinath Rao, *Indian National Movement and Constitutional Development* (Guntur: Sidhartha Printers, 1985), p.4.

people belonging to all castes and creeds, was submitted to the Maharaja on January 1, 1891, popularly known as 'Malayali Memorial'. The partial success of the 'Malayali Memorial' paved the way for the submission of 'Ezhava Memorial', signed by more than thirteen thousand people to the Maharaja in 1896.[5]

The dawn of 20th century witnessed a steady growth of political consciousness in the state of Travancore. The organizations like Indian national congress and Swadeshi Movement started to educate the people on problems facing the country. Being motivated by the new ideas of national democracy, social freedom and equality, people demanded share in the administration. As a result , in 1904, 'Sri Moolam Popular Assembly' was constituted in Travancore where elected members represented the aspirations of the common people.[6] After the first world war people were utterly disappointed over the post-war developments – high prices low wages and shortage of essential commodities. To suppress the unrest of the people government armed itself with drastic powers. People started boycott of foreign goods, non-payment of taxes and agitations were staged. Sree Moolam Assembly which had always been an important forum for focusing popular demand resounded with the cry of responsible government.[7] Disorder, riots and violence permeated the British Indian provinces. In general Kerala kept abreast with other parts of the country, in the demonstration of anti-British feelings, under the impact of growing nationalist consciousness and ideas of democracy and self government. The period under study was thus a time of confusion, unrest

---

[5] K.V.Eapen, *A Study of Kerala History* (Kottyam: Kollett Publications, 1971), pp.297, 298.

[6] G.Sugeetha, "The Constitutional Progress in Travancore in the 19th and 20th centuries", *Journal of Kerala Studies*, Vol.VIII (December, 1981), p.17.

[7] M.J.Koshy, *Last Days of Monarchy in Kerala*, Trivandrum: Kerala Historical Society, 1973, 2.

and people were eagerly waiting for emancipation- a total change.

The 18th century Kerala society was essentially a feudal one consisting of castes and classes. Caste system, social inequalities, slavery, ozhiyam (Unpaid work) joint family and marumakkathayam etc., were some of the significant characteristics. Caste rules framed by the Brahmin reduced a portion of the population, below the caste of Nadars and Ezhavas, to the status of slaves. Such low castes as the Pulayas, the Parayas, the Kuravas, etc., were treated as slaves by the highborn of Kerala society. Brahmins were the most respected group of people who controlled large tracts of land which belonged to the temples. They were ministers of the Rajas and spiritual preceptors. The Nayars constituted the next important division who were the militia of the land. Ezhavas or Tiyyas, the agricultural labourers, had no share in the civic and political life and were much oppressed by Nayars. The lower classes had no liberty, no right of personal safety and freedom. They were treated in the most inhuman and barbarous manner and subjected to the worst form of tyranny.[8] There were several restrictions with regard to their dress, ornaments, domestic vessels and construction of houses. They were banned from using many roads, from many schools and even from entering temples. Even their sight was pollution to the Hindus of higher class.[9]

Towards the middle of the 19th century India was pulsated with a new life and a new hope which were the manifestations of the western impact on Indian society. "The Protestant missionaries were the first humanists to make genuine efforts to improve the condition of the slaves of Kerala".[10] Their sense of justice was very much aroused when they came across cruel

---

[8] A.Sreedhara Menon, *op.cit.,* p.374.

[9] K.Bernard, *Flashes of Kerala History* (Cochin:K.L.Bernard,1977), p.126.

[10] Lawrence Lopez, *A Social History of Modern Kerala* (Trivandrum: Lawrence Lopez, 1988), 37.

and outrageous practices of slave owners and the total denial of justice to those men in bondage. They said that God's will is that one should love his neighbour as himself and slavery is violating the fundamental law of man's nature. The missionaries of the C.M.S co-operated with the missionaries of L.M.S. in exposing evils of slavery and rousing public opinion against it. "The introduction of English education, the activities of Christian missionaries, the multiplication of printing press and the growth of printing press as a medium of mass communication were some of the important factors which influenced the social and cultural life of the people of India during this period".[11] The abolition of slavery was one of the important steps taken in Malabar, Travancore and Cochin towards the establishment of a new society. In the early decades of 20th century Kerala witnessed a social awakening which was a by-product of socio-religious awakening all over India in the 19th century.

Chattampi Swamikal and Sree Narayana Guru were the two religious reformers who worked for the regeneration of Hindu Society. They saw people groaning with the accomplishments of untouchability, unapproachability and denial of freedom. Sree Narayan Guru founded Sree Narayan Dharma Paripalana Sangham in 1903 to propagate his teachings and to uplift the Ezhava community.[12] The brilliant among the Ezhava community was Dr. Palpu whose selfless efforts for the advancement of his community bore fruit in the long run.[13] The other great social reformers of Ezhava community were C.V.Kunjiraman, Kumaraassan, etc., who tried to irradicate irrational superstitious practices. The western educated Nair youths organized 'Malayali Sabha' to encourage

---

[11] C.V.Cherian, *op.cit.,* p.175.

[12] N.K.Bhaskaran, "The Ezhava Memorial and the Founding of SNDP Yogam" *Journal of Kerala Studies,* Vol.IX (December, 1982), p.247.

[13] Lawrence Lopez, *op.cit.,* p.128.

poor but brilliant students to acquire English education by giving monetary assistance, to reform educational system, to encourage female education, to start technical school and to promote the welfare of Nair community.

The 20th century created an atmosphere of protest, revolt and challenge all over the state. It engendered among the lower castes an awareness of freedom and self-respect and induced them to adopt similar line of action for their advancement. Ayyankali, the leader of the Pulayas of Vengannore, was instrumental for the liberation of this long suppressed community. In 1905 Ayyankali organized 'Sadhu Jana Paripalana Sangham' on the model of SNDP.[14] He started a Malayalam monthly called 'Sadhujana Paripalanam' which drew attention of the enlightened sections of other communities to the indignities and degradation to which untouchable were subjected in Kerala. Sri Vakkom Abdul Khadir Moulavi was a liberal-minded Muslim who tried to refine Muslim community out of its meaningless practices and ceremonies which arrested the growth of the Muslim community. Moulavi published 'AL-Islam' journal for the dissemination of liberal ideas among Muslims.[15] Nambuthiries who had constituted themselves as the intellectual aristocracy came in for a general social reformation because they also came under the spell of western education.

The work of the Christian Missionaries and the spread of western education helped to bring about a radical social change. They promoted education by establishing the establishment of colleges and schools at different places in Kerala. The object sought in teaching was that the learners might be able to learn scripture. The impact of western education upon the people of Kerala had chastening influence on the growth and development of freedom. The great-treasures of the West opened to the people of the country

---

[14] *Ibid.*, p.163.
[15] A.Sreedhara Menon, *op.cit.*, p.388.

which undoubtedly accelerated its growth and cultural development.

1.2.   Revivals in Kerala

Prior to the coming of Pentecostal missionaries in the 20th century, there were revivals in Kerala. In the 19th century there was a great awakening in churches in Kerala. These revival movements gave spiritual insight and the arrival of Pentecostal missionaries strengthened the revival and ultimately it lead to the establishment of Pentecostal churches in Kerala.

Till the 19th century Christians in Kerala did not have a copy of the Bible in their language. The Malayalam New Testament was published in 1829 and the whole Bible in 1841 by the efforts of missionaries. As a result of reading the scripture and learning from missionaries, a reform movement started in the churches of Travancore which was mainly led by Abraham Malpan.[16] Mathews Mar Athanasius (1843-1877), the Metropolitan of Marthoma Church, ordered to set apart time after regular Sunday service for learning and preaching the scripture. In 1864, he permitted Ammal, the daughter of a famous convert, Vedanayaka Sastri, to visit his churches and inspire the people to true Christian life with her wonderful Christian songs.[17] Thus the ground for great revival was prepared by the year 1870.

The person who was used as an instrument to bring forth revival in Travancore was John Christian Arulappan,[18] a native

---

[16] K.K.Kuruvilla, *Keralathile Almiya Unarve* (Malayalam) [Spiritual revival in Kerala], (Tiruvalla: Malayalam Christian Literature Committee, 1942), p.34.

[17] K.K.Kuruvilla, *A History of the Marthoma Church and its Doctrines* (Madras: CLS, 1951), p.47.

[18] John Christian Arulappan,who came under the influence of A.N.Groves in 1934 established autonomous assemblies in Tinneveli area resolved to accept no salary but to trust God to provide for all

of Tinneveli. He was a renowned revivalist and independent, itinerant preacher who visited Travancore in the years 1853 and 1859 and conducted revival meetings and attracted large gatherings.[19] The most significant impact of these meetings was an outbreak of the revival among the indigenous Christians. The Metropolitan, Mathews Mar Athanasius supported the reform movements in the church and acted towards the movement sympathetically. Prayer meetings were continuing through out Kerala from 1860's to 1870's. Revival began in Mavelikkara and Tiruvalla.[20] Mathai Upadeshi and Arulappan visited Travancore in 1873, conducted revival meetings in different places at central Travancore became an immediate cause for revival. Arulappan's name appears in the first published account of the revival of Travancore.

A visit of some Arulappan's followers was the immediate cause of excitement in the South. Madras Church missionary record for December 1873, describes the revival in Travancore under the heading signs of a Religious Awakening of Travancore. It describes that the revival movement confined to the district lying between Kottayam and Quilon in which missionary labour has been most concentrated.[21] The themes of their preaching were the crucifixion of Christ, second coming, rule of anti-Christ, millennium, eternal life etc.

As a result of these meetings people got eagerness to read the scriptures. They gave importance to the spiritual needs and less interested in worldly pleasures. The most prominent

---

his needs, a principle which Groves himself had already adopted. K.J.Newton, *Glimpses of Indian Church History* (India: Living Light Publications, 1975), 53.

[19] C.M.Agur, *Church History of Travancore*, New Delhi: Asian Education Service, 1990 (first published in 1903), pp.918,919.

[20] J.Edwin Orr, *Evangelical Awakenings in India in the Early twentieth Century* (New Delhi: Masihi Sahitya Sanstha, 1970), p.35.

[21] W.S.Hunt, *The Anglican Church in Travancore and Cochin 1816-1916* (Kottayam: Church Missionary Society, 1920). p.154.

among those who revived in these meetings were Justus Joseph, a CMS minister and his brothers.[22] Nine CMS congregations and thirteen of the Syrian churches were affected by the revival.[23] Justus Joseph and his brothers spread the awakening to the churches in Kaneeti, Thevalakkara, Njakkannal, Krishnapuram, Puthuppally, Mankuzhi, Kattanam and Cheppad.[24] Later Justus Joseph was excommunicated and his licence was cancelled because his teaching was deviated from the Bible. The event declined the revival movement for a short period.

The work of Lakshmana Rao, a famous revivalist among Marthomities helped to kindle the flame of revival again. Baringgold and Carny were invited to the CMS churches in Travancore to conduct meetings. J.H.Bishop and archdeacon John Caley invited Thomas Walker, a CMS missionary to preach in CMS churches and many Jacobites attended those meetings. Strengthened by those revivals, Marthoma Evangelistic Association was formed in 1888. By the zeal of this association, the revival was spread to the whole church. All these helped to start a fresh revival around the year 1894.[25] The second wave of revival also came to Kerala from Tamilnadu. The important men, who were used for the revival around 1894 were V.D.David (Popular by the name Tamil David) and L.M.Wordsworth from Ceylon. It marked a new chapter in the history of Travancore.[26] As a result of these

---

[22] Sadhu Kochukunju, 'Malankara Sabhayum Almiya Unarvum' (Malayalam) [Church in Malabar and spiritual revival], Kottayam: CMS Press, 1924. Cited in Mathew Daniel, *Sadhu Kochukunjupadesi* (Malayalam) [a short biography of Sadhu Kochukunja] (Tiruvalla: CLS,1988), pp.101-103.

[23] C.M.Agur, *op.cit.*, p.1013.

[24] K.K.Kuruvill, *Keralathile Almiya Unarve*, pp.37-41.

[25] *Ibid.*, pp.47-48.

[26] T.A.Kurian, *Mahakavi K.V.Simon* (Malayalam) [K.V.Simon, the Great Poet], (Angamali: Premier Printers, 1990), p.60.

meetings ten thousand people were converted within the period of three months. In Tamil David's meeting Central Travancore witnessed the confession of sins, with great brokenness and weeping and public witnessing of faith in Christ. David and Wordsworth encouraged to start a convention and C.P. Philipose as the chief organizer, the Maramon Convention was started in 1895. Tamil David preached to the gathering of about 25,000 in that convention.[27] Preaching of David was full of examples and illustrations, very forceful and clear. He had the ability to arrest the attention of the people. He was courageous and able to answer diligently the questions raised by the opponents.[28] He could attract large audiences and won more than any other missionaries did before. His evangelistic addresses were of the simplest style devoid of theological terms.[29]

Bishop of Trichur, while commenting about the mission of two Tamil evangelists made a comparison with European missionaries says, "They knew also how to address their fellow countrymen, infinitely better than Europeans. They knew what their peculiar sins and temptations were. Their illustrations were usually drawn from home life, pointed and pithy."[30] Though Tamil David and Wordsworth were well accepted by the evangelical folk at first, their subsequent visits were not warmly welcomed. T.G.Oomen observes: In 1908 Tamil David came to Kerala as baptized person and a member of Brethren Church.[31] This might have been the reason for

---

27 J.Edwin Orr, *op.cit.*, p.96

28 K.V.Simon, *Malankarayile Verpadu Sabhakalude Charithram* (Malayalam) [History of the Brethran Churches in the Kerala], (Kumbanad: Noyar Memorial Printing House, 1938), p.43.

29 C.M.Agur, *op.cit.*, p.185.

30 *Ibid.*, p.87.

31 T.G.Oommen, *IPCyum Anpathu Varshathe Sevanacharithravum* (Malayalam) [IPC and its fifty years service], (Mallappally: Mallappally Printers,1979), p. 5.

not getting the well acceptance as they had in their previous visits.

Next important revival in Kerala was the revival in the beginning of the 20th century. It was a greatest evangelical awakening and a nation-wide movement. The news of 1904 revival in Wales created profound interest in Trivandrum and held prayer for an outpouring of the Spirit upon India. In Cochin, Kottayam and Kunnamkulam prayer meetings were held for intercession for worldwide revival. Preparation for the 1905 awakening was mainly missionary but as soon as the revival broke out, the great majority of participants and the greater number of leaders were Indians. According to W.A.Stanton "...revival was an answer to the united and persistent prayer, prayer not of the missionaries only, but of the natives..."[32]

As a result of the prayer for the revival in India many native evangelists and preachers experienced the baptism of the Holy Spirit. There were people who dance with spiritual happiness in the revival meetings and it was advised not to hinder it.[33] V.P.Mammen has rightly pointed out that four common features of this revival were deep consciousness of sin, happiness in the Holy Spirit, concern for the unsaved fellow beings and zealous witness for Jesus Christ. People spend time in Bible reading, devotion, do good actions and be filled with Holy Spirit.[34]

Punchamannil Mammen and Moothanpackal Kochukunju were instrumental in further strengthening of the revival. In 1904 Mammen Upedeshi received call from God and he

---

[32] Quoted, Edwin Orr, *op.cit.*, p.151.

[33] "Editorial" (Malayalam), *Malankara Sabha Tharaka* [Star of Malabar Church],4/4 (September, 1907): p.44.

[34] V.P.Mammen, "Nammude Sabhayile Unarve" (Malayalam), [Revival of Our Church], Malankara Sabha Tharaka: 4/4 (October, 1970), p.78.

began to conduct meetings in Kizhakenmuthoor, Tiruvalla, Venmony, Kottarakkara, Chengannur and Kunnamkulam.[35] In these meetings there were much conviction of sin, repentance, weeping and confessing. He also visited Malayalam speaking churches in Madras. These two preachers were very powerful and large crowds attended their meetings. Many people accepted Jesus as their personal saviour. K.E.Abraham, the founder of Indian Pentecostal Church of God, dedicated his life to the Lord's ministry, in one of the meetings conducted by Kochukunju Upadeshi in Pennukara Marthoma Church in 1914.[36]

Malankara Sabha Tharaka reported the news of the revival spread over every nook and corner. Revival took place even in Sunday School classes. In Mavelikkara, a youth gathered some children and started a prayer and it resulted in revival. Being convinced of their sins they began to cry and those gathered by hearing their voice also experienced repentance. Then onwards, daily prayers were conducted and were attended by people from Puthiyakavu and Thazhakara forgetting their denominational differences.[37] Though these revival activities had been mostly held in Travancore, other parts of Kerala also felt its influence.

The missionaries noticed that in the 1905 revival independence of native church was stressed. Men who were formerly the agents and employees of the missionaries began to carry the gospel to the villages with the possibility of extending self-government, self-support and self-propagation.

---

[35] T.P.Abraham, Naveekaranam-Thudakkavum Thudarchayum (Malayalam) [Revival-beginning and continuation], Kottayam: The Ashram Press, 1985,142.cf.J.Edwin Orr, *op.cit.*, p.98.

[36] K.E.Abraham, *Yesukristuvinte Eliya Dasan Atava Pastor K.E.Abraham* (Malayalam) [A humble servant of Jesus Christ or Pastor K.E.Abraham], 2nd ed., Kumbanad: K.E.Abraham Foundation, 1983, pp.16, 17.

[37] "Pathradhipa Kurippukal" (Malayalam) [editorial notes], Malankara Sabha Tharaka, Vol.IV, No.5 (October, 1907), p.74.

This revival was indigenous in character and it was marked by a rising of Asian ministers and laymen to fuller responsibility. The local revival stirred up many natives to reach their neighbours with the good news. The revival resulted in the formation of National Missionary Movement and it reacted as a spiritual force, carrying with it a revival of evangelistic impulse. As Indian nationalism developed an Indian National Christian Council emerged. It is no doubt that 1905 awakening was the beginning of the preparation of the Indian Church and Indian independence.[38]

As a result of learning the scripture revival occurred in the nineteenth century and it helped to the large sale of scriptures and people showed great eagerness to read the word of God. The emphasis of a transforming, regenerating change as a necessary condition to enter into the Kingdom of God[39] resulted in genuine repentance, open confession, and immediate restitution. The outcome of the movement was seen in the ending of all animosities, the settling of social quarrels and reconciling of congregational disputes, even former enemies united in prayer and preaching. It had also greatly affected the social life of the people. People asked forgiveness even to their slaves and had food along with them[40] many spiritual activities were also initiated in the church during this period. Most important among them was the formation of 'Evangelistic Association' and Sunday school. Preaching and Bible reading were made compulsory.[41] Thus the revivals produced a tremendous awakening of the Christian way of life among the masses.

---

[38] J.Edwin Orr., *op.cit.*, pp.157, 158.

[39] K.T.Joy, *The Mar Thoma Church: A Study of Its Growth And Contribution*, Kottayam: K.T.Joy, 1983, p.64.

[40] W.S.Hunt, *op.cit.*, p.158.

[41] M.A.Thomas, *An Outline History of Christian Churches and Denominations in Kerala* (Trivandrum: M.A.Thomas, 1997), 111, 112, cf.F.E.Keay, *A History of the Syrian Church in India* (Delhi: ISPCK 1960), pp.96, 97.

1.3.   Brethren Movement

Brethren churches established in Kerala at the eve of the 20th century became a forerunner to the Pentecostal movement in Kerala. Mr.Gregson, the first missionary of the Brethren movement, came to Kerala in 1896 and obtained permission from the Metropolitan to work among the Marthomites in Kerala. Even though Mar Thoma Church lost all her properties by the court judgment in 1889, it sustained by repeated revivals and they encouraged evangelistic preaching. So they did not find it difficult to invite Mr. Gregson to preach in Maramon convention of 1897. Gregson, who taught "The Epistles to the Colossians" and "Romans" in one month course on the Bible , in September 1898, emphasized on the believer's baptism and due to this reason his entry was restricted in the Marthoma churches.[42] Therefore he began to work independently. A small group attracted by his teachings joined with him and the first Brethren Church was formed at Kumbanad in 1898. P.E.Mammen, a priest in the Marthoma Church who had salvation experience at the meetings of Tamil David in 1894, accepted the Brethren teaching and baptized at Kunnamkulam in 1899 by a missionary named Baired.[43] Mr.Nagal, who was working in the Basel Mission joined the Brethren Movement and published a book 'Christian Baptism', that made a sensation among the reformed ones and many followed the new teaching. K.V. Simon, who had attended the revival meetings held by Tamil David and Wordsworth learned the scripture and by reading many articles and books got convinced of Brethren teaching. Thus he was baptized in December 28, 1902 and gave active leadership for the Brethren Movement in Kerala.[44] By 1906 Brethren work gained momentum and many churches were established.

---

[42] K.V.Simon, *op.cit.,* p.56.
[43] T.G.Oommen, IPC yum ...*op.cit.,* p.5.
[44] T.A.Kurian, *op.cit.,* p.117.

K.V.Simon and his friends organized a movement, called *'Viyojithan'* (Separatists) in 1914, when the suggestion to the Brethren missionaries for a few reforms, remained unheeded.[45] Another division occurred in 1921, owing to the issue of missionary dominance. When a land was purchased for the church, it was decided to form a trust. Noyal wanted to form the trust with missionaries as members while P.E.Mammen demanded to elect members from the natives. They could not come to an agreement so the group led by Noyal was known as 'Open Brethren' and the group led by P.E.Mammen was known as Syrian Brethren.[46] P. E. Mammen published many tracts pointing out the independence of the church with scriptural evidences.[47] It later influenced the natives to strive for the native leadership.

1.4.   Indian Christians' Struggle against Missionary Control

Christianity is a missionary religion, which sent missionaries to different parts of the world from the beginning of the era to preach the gospel and to establish churches. Following the period of reformation we find some revival in the field of missionary work. Since seventeenth century we find active missionary work in the lands which were conquered by the West. According to Sebastian Vadakel various circumstances and factors such as colonization of the far away lands by the European countries contributed their share to the origin of missionary societies in the 17th century. The missionary activity was then organized and directed by the colonial powers, especially by Spain and Portugal who enjoyed the patronage right.[48] According to J.W.Gladstone Roman Catholic missions

---

[45] K.V.Simon, *op.cit.*, pp.193, 194.

[46] E.J.Chacko, *Keralathile Chila Swathanthra Sabhakal* (Malayalam) [Some Independent Churches in Kerala], (Tiruvalla: TLC, 1986), p.12.

[47] K.E.Abraham, Ysukristhuvinte *...op.cit.*, p.80.

[48] Sebastian Vadakel, *An Indigenous Missionary Endeavour*, (Vadavathoor: OIRSI, 1990), pp.30, 31.

were very active in South India after the arrival of the Jesuits who worked under the patronage of Portuguese. As a result of their work in Coastal areas of Kerala, many fisher men were converted to Christianity.[49] Evangelical revivals in England, the USA and other countries of the West, helped to establish a number of Missionary Societies. The most important among them are SPCK (1698), SPG (1701), BMS (1792), LMS (1795), CMS(1799) etc.[50] Almost all the missionary societies sent their missionaries to the places practising other faiths, lands including India. It helped greatly to the expansion of Christianity in the 19th century.

Many missionary societies had been working in Kerala too. The LMS, CMS, and Basel Mission were the early missionary societies to have unbroken activities. They have mainly concentrated their work in the Southern, Central, and Northern part of Kerala respectively. Their work had brought many changes in Kerala. The change in the policy of British East India Company in 1833 helped much to the progress of missionary work in the 19th century.

Thus 19th century was a period of great missionary expansion and also the great age of colonialism. Almost all the churches established by the Western missionaries were under the control of the mission bodies till the middle of the 20th century. "... Rising spirit of nationalism and the early movements against British domination led to an anti-missionary feeling for many who shared the spirit of nationalism."[51] Christians also began to raise their voice against the domination of missionaries over the church. Missionaries did not like to have an Indian to be appointed in any official position of the church. The revolt of the Indian Christians against the dominance of the missionaries was an

---

[49] J.W.Gladstone, *Protestant Christianity and People's Movement in Kerala 1850-1936* (Trivandrum: Seminary Publications, 1984), p.57.

[50] C.B.Firth, *An Introduction to Indian Church History*, (Madras: CLS, 1983), pp.131,145.

[51] J.W.Gladstone, *op.cit.*, p.310.

outcome of the acceptance of the Gospel as a source for a new identity. Missionaries provided many Indians with an education which infused in them a new sense of human possibilities. They felt that the missionaries were hindering them from realizing the implications of the Gospel and maturing themselves as responsible persons. One of the recurrent themes on which Indian leaders spoke at the missionary conferences in India during the second half of the nineteenth century was the domination and humiliating attitude of the missionaries towards the Indians, especially towards the Indian clergymen.[52]

Lal Behari Day who started a movement against the exclusive missionary control of the church in 1850's, advocated that Indian ordained ministers should be put on an equal footing with the missionaries and have the right of membership in the church council.[53] K.M.Banerjee, as president of the Bengal Christian Association organized in the seventies of the 19th century to develop autonomy of the church from western missions.[54] He expressed his vision of an Indian Church at the third Decennial Missionary Conference held at Bombay in 1892-1893. ... "The native church in India should be *one*, not divided; *native*, not foreign."[55]

Missionaries like Henry Venn and Rufus Anderson advocated the need for the development of indigenous leadership in the Anglican Church.[56] As the chief secretary

---

[52] George Thomas, *Christian Indians and Indian Nationalism 1885-1950. An Interpretation in Historical and Theological perspectives* D.Th Dissertation, University of Hamburg, 1979(Unpublished), pp.68, 69.

[53] A.Mathias Mundadan, *Indian Christians Search for Identity and Struggle for Autonomy* (Bangalore: Dharmaram Publications, 1984), p.169.

[54] M.M.Thomas and P.T.Thomas, *Towards an Indian Christian Theology,* (Tiruvalla: New Day Publications 1992), p.23.

[55] *Quoted,* M.K.Kuriakose, *History of Christianity in India: Source Materials,* (Madras: CLS, 1982), 252.

[56] Stephen Neill, *The Story of the Christian Church in India and Pakistan,* Madras: CLS-ISPCK, 1972), pp.156, 157.

of the Church Missionary Society from 1841 to 1872, Henry Venn desired to the formation of self-governing independent national churches in every Country. According to the Church Council system he introduced the missionaries should handover the authority and responsibilities of the church to national leadership and move to a new area where there are no Christians.[57] In 1874 South Travancore Church Council was formed. Many such attempts were made to develop a native leadership among the LMS and CMS circles. But the missionaries continued to be 'masters' and the Indian pastors were considered as their 'native agents'.[58] According to T.V.Philip, consciousness of an Indian Church began to take root among the Indian Christians only after the growth of the national movement.[59] At the beginning of the 20th century, Indians attempted to evangelize India without the help of foreign missionaries. On 25th December 1905 National Missionary Society of India was formed to evangelize India, with Indian men, Indian money and the Indian management.[60]

Early in the 20th century, there were serious discussions among the LMS circles concerning the appointment of Indians as leaders. The 1921 Travancore Church Council meeting decided to appoint an Indian as chairman of Nagercoil district.[61] The church in Nagercoil District has grown as an Indian was in charge of it. George Parker and Philips in 1933 emphasized the fact that unnecessary foreign appearance is a hindrance to Christianity in India and that Christianity must be rooted in Indian soil and grow gradually more Indians in its spirit as well as in its outward forms and this process would

---

[57] T.P.Abraham and Mar Aprem (eds.), "Venn, Rev.Henry" *Sabha Charithra Nigandu* (Malayalam) [Dictionary of the Christian Church], (Tiruvalla: TLC, 1986), pp.324, 325.

[58] J.W.Gladstone, *op.cit.*, p.323.

[59] T.V.Philip, *Ecumenism in Asia* (Tiruvalla: CSS-ISPCK, 1994), pp.92.

[60] V.S.Azariah, *India and Missions* (London: CLS, 1909), p.95.

[61] John A.Jacob, *A History of LMS in South Travancore 1806-1959* (Nagercoil: Diocean Press, 1990), p.213.

be assisted if the official head of each district is an Indian.[62] In period between 1912 to 1930 Indians were consecrated as bishops in Anglican, Roman Catholic and Methodist churches. V.S.Azariah was consecrated in 1912 as Bishop of Anglican Church, Mgr. Tiburtius Roche in 1923 as Roman Catholic Bishop and J.R.Chitambar as Methodist Bishop in 1930.[63] Anglican Church in India, formerly a branch of the Church of England became independent in 1930, managing its own affairs in its own Episcopal Synod and General Council.[64] Thus among the protestant churches in India there were a considerable progress in 20th century towards a self-supporting, self-governing and self-propagating church, particularly since the first World War.[65] Among the Protestant churches this was a period of transition from missionary leadership to native leadership. Struggle in the main line churches during the formative period of the Pentecostal churches influenced greatly to work for native leadership.

The Reforming party among the Thomas Christians [Syrian Christians] did not like to leave the Syrian Church and join with the missionaries[66] working in Kerala during the nineteenth century, clearly points the unwillingness of the Thomas Christians to accept the missionary dominance. Thomas Mar Athanasius was able to establish the church firmly as an independent autonomous church.[67] Titus Varghese observes: "Reformed party stood for freedom from ecclesiastical domination."[68] According to K.K.Kuruvilla, church under foreign missionary leadership and its dependence on foreign money is an obstacle

---

[62] *Ibid.* p.216.

[63] Stephen Neill, *op.cit.,* pp.155,156.

[64] M.E.Gibbs, *From Jerusalem to New Delhi,* (Madras: CLS, 1978), p.275.

[65] C.B.Firth, *op.cit.,* p.261.

[66] Juhanon Mar Thoma, *Christianity in India and a Brief History of the Mar Thoma Syrian Church,* rev.4th ed. (Madras: K.C.Cherian,1968), p.23.

[67] Mar Aprem, *Indian Christian Directory,* Bangalore (Bangalore Parish of the Church of the East, 1984), p.104.

[68] V.Titus Varghese and P.P.Philip, *Glimpses of the History of the Christian Churches in India,* (Madras, CLS, 1983), p.117.

to its progress.[69] Thus the reformed party without joining the foreign missionaries progressed under native leadership. After the separation of reformed party known as Mar Thoma Syrian Church, at the beginning of 20th century Orthodox Syrian Church had a desire to obtain the autonomous status for the development of the church, approached patriarch of Antioch to institute a catholicate for the church in India. Patriarch Addulla did not grant the request, but demanded registered documents from the bishop acknowledging his supremacy at his visit to Kerala in 1909. Dissatisfied in his decision, Catholicate was created in September 1912 and Syrian Orthodox Church obtained a native leadership.[70] According to C.B.Firth "It was a move to secure full local autonomy."[71] It shows that there was a struggle among the Syrian Christians to come under the native leadership.

From the middle of the 19th century a large group desired to free the church from the foreign missionary control. The rising spirit of nationalism compelled many missionaries to think in the same way, attempted to give opportunities to the Indians too. Thus in the beginning of 20th century we find attempts to transfer the power and responsibilities from the missionaries to the natives. This transition of power also influenced the Pentecostals too to demand for an Indian leadership.

Since it was a period of struggle for national independence, and the Protestant churches as well as the Thomas Christians argued for the Indian leadership, it also influenced the early native leaders to stand for the indigenous leadership. Missionaries who disliked such an attempt were not ready to handover the responsibilities to the natives. Therefore, divisions occurred among the Pentecostals when they struggled for the native leadership.

---

[69] K.K.Kuruvilla, *Bharathathile Kraisthava Sabhakal Oru Samshipta Charithram* (Malayalam) [A brief history of Christian churches in India], (Tiruvalla: CLS, n.d.), pp.265, 266.

[70] Mar.Aprem., *op.cit.*, pp.77-78.

[71] C.B.Firth, *op.cit.*, p.179.

CHAPTER II

Origin of Pentecostal Churches and the Emergence of Indigenous Leadership

Pentecostals, Christians with some distinctive characteristics, claim that their teachings are rooted in the Bible.[1] The mainline churches consider the Pentecostals as a sect[2] or cult because they establish new denominations in protest against the paralyzing chill that seems to have overtaken the traditional churches in its compromise with the world. According to Horton Davies, the movement is a salutary reminder that Christianity is a missionary and heart-warming faith.[3] The growth of Pentecostalism in this period has been phenomenal and it has affected many in the traditional churches in the United States of America and Europe. In Italy Pentecostals outnumber all other Protestants. Pentecostals are fast growing in Africa and Latin America and a fifth of the voters in Brazil and Chile belong to Pentecostal denominations.[4] According to Steven J. Land, Pentecostalism is largely a Third World

---

[1] M.Stephen, "The Challenge of the Pentecostal Churches Today: an Insider's View", *Jeevadhara* 25/148 (July, 1995): p.274.

[2] 'Sect' is defined as a movement of reaction, the followers of which are very much personally engaged.Nills Bloch Hoell, *The Pentecostal Movement: Its Origin, Development and Distinctive Character* (London: George Allen & Unwin Ltd., 1964), p.69.

[3] Horton Davies, *The Challenge of the Sects* (London: SCM Press, 1963), p.84.

[4] Harold E.Fey, *A History of Ecumenical Movement* Vol.II, 2nd.ed., (Geneva: WCC, 1986), p.382.

Movement and there is a growing tendency among the Pentecostals to start indigenous churches. The non-white, world-wide indigenous Pentecostals were estimated in 1970 as 60% and it reached to 75% by 1985.[5] Pentecostals have shown more cultural adaptability than any other Christian groups. They have sensed the differences between theology and culture and generally have been successful in creating indigenous churches which incorporate unique local cultural forms.[6]

The Pentecostals believe that they have returned basically to the New Testament patterns of doctrine, religious experience and practice. Though the church's methods, organization and general approach to the world vary according to the local cultures, they hold the view that the doctrines and religious experiences of the apostles are constant standards for every age, and that should not change.[7] Therefore the Pentecostals do not consider themselves as a group originated in the twentieth century with a new set of beliefs but claim their origin back to the first century, when the supernatural gifts of the spirit was exercised.[8]

2.1.   Origin of Modern Pentecostal Movement

Modern Pentecostal Movement which sprang out at the very beginning of the twentieth century is considered as an offshoot of Holiness Movement in the latter half of the 19th century that stem down from Wesleys' teachings on Christian

---

[5] Steven J.Land, "Pentecostal Spirituality: Living in the Spirit" Louis Dupre and Don E.Saliers (eds.) *World Spirituality, An Encyclopedic History of the Religious Quest: Vol.III, Christian Spirituality Post Reformation and Modern,* (New York: The cross road publishing company, 1991), p.482.

[6] P.B.Thomas, "Pentecostal Ecclesiology: Promises and Problems", *Jeevadhara* Vol.XX, (1990): p.295.

[7] David J.DuPlessis, "The Historic Background of Pentecostalism" *One in Christ,* Vol.X., (1974): pp.175, 176.

[8] Steve Durasoff, *Bright Wind of the Spirit: Pentecostalism Today,* (New Jersey: Logos International, 1972), p.15.

perfection in the 18th century.[9] In the last quarter of nineteenth century, there were a number of incidents in which tongues did break out. So the emergence of Pentecostalism in the next century may be seen as a natural development of forces that had been set in motion much earlier.[10] Such events happened not only in the eighteenth and nineteenth century but throughout the centuries. Bernad Bresson in his book *"Studies in Ecstasy"* gives a list of about twenty four charismatic movements and sects manifested from the time of Montanus in second century to the middle of the nineteenth century.[11] But the charismatic manifestations occurred prior to 1900 isolated and episodic in nature.[12] Revivals were occurred at various parts of the world during this period viz., Armenia, Wales, South India and United States. It is not easy to ascribe the origin of the movement to a particular place or a person.

One of the first major revivals at the turn of the century occurred in Bethel Bible College at Topeka, Kansas in USA. Since many Holiness groups claim different proofs for the baptism in the Holy Spirit, Parham, a Holiness preacher, assigned his students to find out the biblical evidence of baptism in the Holy Spirit. They found out 'speaking in tongues' as the only evidence for it and Parham asked to pray for it. As a result of continuous prayer to the experience described in the book of Acts, Agnez N.Ozman first received baptism in the Holy

---

[9] Melvin E.Dieter, "Wesleyan-Holiness Aspects of Pentecostal Origins: As Mediated Through the Nineteenth-Century Holiness Revival", Vinson Synan (ed.), *Aspects of Pentecostal Charismatic Origins* (New Jersey: Logos International, 1975) p.59.

[10] Donald W.Dayton, "From Christian Perfection to the Baptism of the Holy Ghost", Vinson Synan (ed.), *Aspects of Pentecostal Charismatic Origins, op.cit.,* pp.51, 52.

[11] Bernard Bresson, *Studies in Ecstacy* (New York: Vantage Press, 1966), pp.20-112.

[12] Williams W.Menzies, *Anointed to Serve: A Story of the Assemblies of God* (Missouri: Gospel Publishing House, 1971), p.33.

Spirit. Parham also received this experience, and along with twelve other students and they propagated this teaching in Texas and Missouri.[13]

W.J.Seymour, a Black Holiness preacher and a student of Parham, was used for the Azusa Street revival which began in 1906, and it continued for three years. People from America, Europe, and third world countries received baptism in the Holy Spirit and they spread the teaching in different countries.[14] Within a short period, the Pentecostalism spread outward from the revival on Azusa Street and became a third force in Christendom.[15] According to Leonard Lovett both Parham and Seymour share equal position as founders of modern Pentecostalism. Parham laid the doctrinal foundation of the movement, while Seymour served as the catalytic agent for its popularization.[16]

The participants of Azusa Street revival considered their new found tongues to be the languages of the world given to fill in the evangelization of heathen countries.[17] Though the leaders of the revival did not organize any missionary society, the enthusiasm for world evangelization inspired – men and women, clergy and laity, blacks and whites – to set out as missionaries overseas. As completely directed by the spirit many individuals, recently equipped with the power of the Holy Spirit, propagated the Pentecostal faith in the foreign lands, without depending on the support of any human

---

[13] Steve Durasoff, *op.cit.*, pp.56, 57.

[14] Walter J.Hollenweger, *The Pentecostals* (London: SCM Press Ltd.)1972, p.22.

[15] Vinson Synan, *The Holiness Pentecostal Movement in United States,* (Grand Rapids: Eerdmans Publishing Company, 1971), p.215.

[16] Leonard Lovett, "Black Origins of the Pentecostal Movement", Vinson Synan (ed.), *Aspects of Pentecostal Charismatic Origins, op.cit.,* p.136.

[17] W.F.Carothers, *The Baptism with the Holy Ghost and the Speaking in Tongues,* Illinois: Carothers, 1907, p.21.

agencies.[18] Thus A.G.Garr, one of the participants of Azusa Street revival, traveled first to India and then to China, remained abroad learning language and culture of the people whom he wished to evangelize. T. K. Barret, a pastor of the Methodist Episcopal Church in Norway, received baptism in the spirit at Los Angeles during his visit to United States in 1906, propagated Pentecostalism in Sweden, Denmark, Finland and Germany.[19] He spent about nine months during 1908-09 and through his ministry many of the missionaries working in India received baptism in the Holy Spirit.[20] Prominent among them are Bouncil, Aldivingle and Christian Schoonmaker. Concerning the ministry of Barret and Garr at Coonoor in South India, Christian Schoonmaker writes:

> "During the summer of 1908, a number of Missionaries went to Coonoor, South India for their holidays. Thomas Barret of Norway had been invited to join us... A brother and sister Garr from the Azusa Street meeting in California were also with us. Several missionaries were seeking baptism and one after another was filled, sometimes after days of earnest prayer...."[21]

Later some organizations and missionary societies were formed and more missionaries were set out to propagate the gospel in foreign lands through their own initiative or with the encouragement of these agencies. But the foreign missionary enterprises were more strengthened by the formation of the General Council of the Assemblies of God in 1914, Pentecostal Church of God in 1919, and Pentecostal

---

[18] Gary B.McGee, "The Azusa Street Revival and Twentieth Century Missions" *International Bullettin of Missionary Research* (April, 1988): p.59.

[19] Elmer Louis Moon, *The Pentecostal Church: A History of Popular Survey* (New York: Carlton Press, 1966), p.16

[20] Nills Bloch Hoell, *The Pentecostal Movement: Its Origin, Development and Distinctive Character* (London: George Allen & Unwin Ltd., 1964), p.69.

[21] Christians Schoonmaker, *A Man Who Loved the Will of God*, Missouri: AG Foreign (Mission Department, 1959), p.14.

Assemblies of God in 1919, and the Foursquare Gospel in 1923.[22] Along with many independent missionaries, the missionaries sent by the General Council of Assemblies of God, and Church of God, Cleveland, Tennessee were used to establish many churches in Kerala.

2.2.   Revival in Mukti Mission, Pune

Prior to the coming of A.G.Garr and Thomas Barret in 1908, the outpouring of the Holy Spirit occurred in India, which was at Mukti Mission. Though the manifestation of the Holy Spirit occurred many times in different revivals in South India during the latter part of the 19th century, most of them did not emerge as a movement that continue for long. But the revival occurred at Mukti Mission in 1905 identified as the first Pentecostal Movement in India. Pandita Ramabai, a Brahmin convert to Christianity in 1883, opened a home for widows and orphans called Saradha Sadan in 1889 which later came to be known as 'The Ramabhai Mukti Mission'.[23] As one who attended the Keswik convention in 1898 and inspired by the reports of the Australian and Welsh revival in 1903 and 1904, she organized special prayer sessions among the inmates of Mukti Mission for similar revival.[24] About seventy girls out of the hundreds at Mukti Mission volunteered to join the prayer band,[25] and on 29th June 1905, a revival broke out at the mission. About it Ramabai herself writes:

> "One Sunday as I was coming out of the Church, after the morning service, I saw some girls standing…greatly excited and wondering.   …A girl was praying aloud, and praising God in the English language. She did not know the language

---

[22] Gary B.McGee, *op.cit.*, p.59.

[23] C.B.Firth, *An Introduction to Indian Church History*, (Madras: CLS, 1983), pp.194, 195.

[24] Helen S.Dyer, *Revival in India*, (London: Margon & Scott, 1907), p.43.

[25] Minnie F.Abrams, "How Pentecost Came to India", *The Pentecostal Evangel.* (May, 1945), p.5.

... She was perfectly unconscious of what she was speaking to the Lord Jesus very fluently in English ...."[26]

Minnie F.Abrams, an eye-witness of the revival in the Mukti Mission says:

"Our girls and boys and workers pray in unknown tongues during these sessions of simultaneous prayer, ...The praise and intercession in unknown tongues are full of power. A few have given address in unknown tongues giving the interpretation sentence by sentence. Some have spoken in unknown tongues to others to whom the gift have been given by the Holy Spirit, interpreting for them."[27]

She describes the experience, quaking and shaking their body as Quakers did formerly and Holy Spirit shakes them at his pleasure. Clapping hands and rolling on the floor were also witnessed on certain occasions.[28] As in the case of revival in South India, at Mukti too there was a strong conviction of sins. About it Manorabai writes:

"...strong conviction of sin and deep sorrow for it were given. A realization of the awfulness of sin, and a dread of its results took possession of many. And in almost all parts of Mukti ... at all times of the day, souls crying to God for mercy and forgiveness. Quarrels were put away and things wrong in the lives were put right."[29]

The 20th century revival did not die down as the other revivals in the early period because it occurred on a world level. The revival in India too kindled by the coming of missionaries,

---

[26] Ramabai, "Showers of Blessings", *Mukti Prayer Bell*, 3/4 (September, 1907), cited in Shamsundar Manohar Adhav, *Pandita Ramabai* (Madras: CLS, 1979), p.219.

[27] Minnie F.Abrams, "Mukti Mission and Revival", *Mukti Prayer Bell*, (September, 1907), Shamsundhar Manohar Adhav, *op.cit.*, p.227.

[28] *Ibid.*

[29] Letter addressed to the Friends by Manorabai, on 8th October 1906, Published in Shamsundar Manohar Adhav, *op.cit.*, p.230.

such as Garr and Barret. Many missionaries belong to Brethren and Evangelical Alliance also got the Pentecostal experience and this revival movement spread all throughout India and especially in South India, where there it got a favourable environment condition for the growth.

2.3.   Early Pentecostal Missionaries

The independent missionaries – George Berg, Robert F.Cook, Bouncil and Aldivingle – began to work in Kerala even before the arrival of any of the Pentecostal missionaries sent by an organization. Since the people were prepared by the different revivals many received Pentecostal teachings and a few congregations were formed. Now we shall turn to the work of some important Pentecostal missionaries and then to the origin and growth of the Pentecostal churches in Kerala.

2.3.1. George Berg

The first Pentecostal missionary who came to Kerala was a German, named George Berg, from Chicago in America. He was a minister of a Protestant Church in Chicago, who received baptism in the Holy Spirit and came to South India in 1908. Berg first came to Travancore in 1909 as a preacher of the Brethren convention held at Trikkannamangal in Kottarakkara.[30] Since the Pentecostal churches were not taken an established form in those days, and Berg was an independent missionary, Brethrens did not find it difficult to invite him to preach in the convention. According to K.E.Abraham:

> "In those days Brethrens also believed that baptism in the Holy Spirit is an experience takes place after re-generation. They too held tarry-meetings to receive that experience. Therefore Brethrens did not find it difficult to invite George Berg to preach in their convention."[31]

---

[30] K.E.Abraham, *Yesukristhuvinte Eliya Dasan Atava Pastor K.E.Abraham* (Malayalam) [Humble servant of Jesus Christ or Pastor K.E.Abraham], (Kumbanad: K.E.Abraham Foundation, 1983), p.60.

[31] *Ibid.*, p.61.

Due to certain disagreements with the missionaries who came in the 1910 Brethren Convention, Berg held meetings independently in different places in Kottarakara and Adoor, which were the first independent Pentecostal gatherings in Kerala. In 1911, Berg came to Travancore along with Charles Commins and at this visit an independent fellowship led by Paruthuppara Oommen[32] at Thuvayoor near Adoor, accepted the teaching of Berg and it became a Pentecostal gathering.[33] Berg and Commins held meetings at Punthala Kidangannoor, Vettiyar, Venmony and Elanthoor in Central Travancore.[34]

Pandalam Mathai and Oommen Mammen accompanied Berg to Bangalore, accepted Pentecostal teaching, and began to proclaim it in Central Travancore when they returned in 1912. Berg went to America to attend the First Worldwide Pentecostal Camp Meeting in California in 1912 and returned to South India along with Robert F.Cook.[35] Dora P.Myers observes:

> "Berg loved the people and treated them as equals. Therefore in his days many desired to have fellowship with him. Though there was no mission board to help him and was working independently, the money he received was equally distributed to his co-workers. He set apart a part of his income to help the poor."[36]

---

[32] Paruthuppara Oommen, guided by a special vision went to Thuvayoor, where he began a prayer meeting in the house of Geevarghese Thomas, which continued in relation to the independent Viyojitha group till 1911.

[33] G.Daniel (ed.) "Thuvayoor Daivasabha Kazhinja Ezhupathanju Samvalsarangaliloode" (Malayalam) [Thuvayoor Church of God through the last seventy five years], *Church of God (Full Gospel) in India, Thuvayoor, Platinum Jubilee Souvenir*, Thuvayoor: CGI, 1987, p.8.

[34] K.E.Abraham, *IPC Praramba Varshangal* (Malayalam) [Beginning years of IPC], 2nd ed. (Kumbanad: K.E.Abraham Foundation, 1986), p.8.

[35] Saju, *Kerala Pentecosthu Charithram* (Malayalam) [History of Pentecostal churches in Kerala], (Kottayam: Goodnews Publications, 1994), pp.31, 32.

[36] Dora P.Myers, *Daivasabha Charithram* (Malayalam) [History of Church of God], (Mulakkuzha: Church of God in India, 1960), p.50.

The first congregation in Kerala which accepted Pentecostal teaching was Thuvayoor Church which had an indigenous origin. Berg or anyone who accompanied in his missionary work had no intention to bring the churches under the yoke of westerners. It was purely an independent work.

2.3.2. Robert F.Cook

Robert F. Cook who attended the First World Wide Pentecostal Camp Meeting in California in 1912, heard about India from George Berg who was working in India as a missionary for four years since 1908. Thus Robert F.Cook came along with his wife and two children to South India in 1913 and settled at Dodaballapur near Bangalore. When he found that the work in Travancore is more successful he concentrated his work in Travancore.[37] At his first visit to Travancore in 1914 he could baptize sixty three persons at Thuvayoor. Cook married Bertha Foax in June 1918[38] after the death of his first wife Anna on 31st August, 1917 due to malaria and enteric fever.[39] By his different visits from Dodballapur, near Banglore to Travancore between 1914 to 1921, churches were established at Adoor, Chaliyakkara, Vilakkudy and Punalur, in Central Travancore and he named his churches as Full Gospel Church in Malabar.[40] He became an affiliated missionary of Assemblies of God in 1919 thinking that there should be someone responsible to him, according to the British policy after the First World War and continued this

---

[37] T.M.Varghese and E.V.George, *Anpathu Varshangal* (Malayalam) [Fifty years], Mulakkuzha: CGI Literature Service 1973, p.14.

[38] Robert F.Cook, *Half a Century of Divine Leading and 37 years of Apostolic Achievements in South India,* Tennesse: Church of God Foreign Mission Department, 1955, p.52.

[39] Robert F.Cook, "Death of Sister Cook", *Weekly Evangel* (November, 1917), 7, cf.Divine leadings...*op.cit.,* p.44.

[40] T.M.Varghese and E.V.George, *op.cit.,* pp.24, 25.

relation till 1929.[41] Cook rented a small house at Kottarakkara. He always tried to identify himself with poor people in the society.[42] Cook conducted an annual convention in December 1923 at Arattupuzha before he left for furlough. In his absence, Mr.Charles Commins and Spencer May were in charge of Cook's work. Cook came back to India in 1926 along with Blossom Cook who was also accepted as an affiliated missionary of Assemblies of God. Cook shifted his residence to Kallissery and in 1927 built headquarters at Mulakuzha in Chengannur, where he started a Bible School to train the natives in 1928.[43]

Cook along with the native leaders severed relations with AG in 1929 and began to work without having any relation to foreign mission.[44] The separation of K.E.Abraham from Cook in 1930 was a great blow to his work in Travancore. But he continued his work independently till he joined the Church of God, Cleveland, Tennesse in 1936.[45] Cook served for 14 more years as a missionary of Church of God and was called back to USA in 1950. He breathed his last at the age of 79 at Cleveland, Tennesse in January 12, 1958. Cook was a missionary who came to India at a very early age and

---

[41] Robert F.Cook, "Sabhakariyam" (Malayalam) [Church Matters], *Suvisha Prabhashakan* (August-September, 1929), 4. According to '*A Quarter Century of Divine Leading in India* Published in 1939 Cook became an affiliated missionary of AG in 1920. cf.R.F.Cook, *Quarter Century...* p.57.

[42] Robert F.Cook, Half a Century ... *op.cit.,* pp.98, 99.

[43] T.M.Varghese and E.V.George *op.cit.,* 27, 28. cf. "Bible School" (Malayalam), *Suvisesha Prabashakan,* Vol.II, Nos.10, 11 (May-June, 1929), p.267.

[44] A.C.Samuel, *Assemblies of God* (Malayalam), Trivandrum: The Malayalam District of SIAG, 1954, 24. cf.K.E.Abraham, "Jnangalude Naveena Padhathi" (Malayalam) [Our New Plan] *Suviesha Prabhashakan* 2/12 (July, 1929), pp.269.

[45] Charles.W.Conn, *Like a Mighty Army,* Tennese: Church of God Publishing House, 1955, 236. cf.T.M.Varghese, *op.cit.,* p.29.

spent long time in India. He identified with the people by living and eating with them especially the poor and depressed. He had become an Indian in every aspect while ministering among the Indians.

2.3.3. *Ms. Bouncil and Ms. Aldivingle*

During the period in which George Berg came to India two Brethren missionaries named Ms. Bouncil and Ms.Aldivingle received baptism in the Holy Spirit by the ministry of Thomas Barret at Connoor in 1908.[46] Both of them had visited Kumbanad and Kallissery in Central Travancore as Brethren missionaries previously, accompanied George Berg in his third journey to Travancore in 1911. They concentrated their ministry in Southern part of Travancore and churches were established at Paraniyam, Pulugal, Melappuram, Vallarakkavila, Irenipuram, Plantop and Kulachal. A.C.Mathai co-operated with them. They moved to Tanjore in 1914 and while they were in Tanjore Ms. Bouncil died.[47] Guided by a special vision Aldivingle searched, C.Manasse of Paraniyam and again reached South Travancore. Then onwards, she concentrated her work in South Travancore. Mrs. Mary Chapman, who shifted her residence from Madras to Trivandrum in 1921, worked in co-operation with Aldivingle. By her influence Aldivingle who was working independently, joined the General Council of Assemblies of God.[48] According to Saju:

> "A.C.Mathai, who believed in the freedom of local church and independent, indigenous organization, was not happy to join with Assemblies of God, which had its headquarters abroad"[49]

---

[46] P.D.Johnson, *Vagdatha Nivarthi* (Malayalam) [the promise fulfilled], Trivandrum: P.D.Johnson, 1968, pp.123.

[47] Saju, *op.cit.,* pp.56.

[48] T.S.Abraham, *pentacosthu prasthanam* (Malayalam) [Pentecostal Movement], Kumbanad: Hebron Book Depot, 1969, pp.75, 76.

[49] Saju, *op.cit.,* p.61.

Without taking into consideration A.C.Mathai's displeasure Aldivingle joined the General Council of Assemblies of God.

2.3.4. *Mrs. Mary W.Chapman*

Mrs. Mary W.Chapman, who received baptism in the Holy Spirit in 1904 revival in the United States,[50] was sent as the first official missionary of Assemblies of God. She visited Travancore occasionally and worked in co-operation with other independent missionaries such as Aldivingle and Robert. F. Cook, who were working in south and central part of Kerala respectively. In 1921 she changed her headquarter from Madras to Trivandrum to concentrate her work in Travancore.[51] In 1924 she again changed her residence to Angadickal in Chengannur to extend help to the people badly affected by the flood. In 1925 Mrs.Chapman started publishing a monthly called *'Pentecosthu Kahalam'*. Spencer May was the publisher and A.J.John was its editor. It had a circulation of about 1200 to 1500 copies.[52] During this period many natives joined the Pentecostal Church and the Pentecostal churches were in progress. John.H.Burgess, who came in 1926 stayed along with Mrs.Chapman in Mavelikkara. After a long years of service Mrs. Chapman died on Sunday at 8 pm, on 27th November 1927 at her quarters in Mavelikkara.[53]

Berg, Cook, Bouncil, Aldivingle and Mrs. Chapman were the earliest Pentecostal missionaries who worked in Kerala. They laid the foundation for the Pentecostal work, on the ground which was prepared by the revival in South India.

---

[50] Mary W.Chapman, "Testimony" (Malayalam) *Pentecosthu Kahalam*, 1/1 (November, 1925),16.

[51] Daniel Ayroor, *Keralathile Pentecosthu Subhakal* Vol.I (Malayalam) [Pentecostal Churches in Kerala], Mavelikkara: Beersheba Bible College, 1986, p.45.

[52] John H.Burgess, *Opportunities in South India and Ceylon,* Springfield: General Council of the Assemblies of God, n.d., p.16.

[53] "The Late Missionary Mrs.Mary Chapman" *Pentecosthu Kahalam*, [Pentecostal Trumphet] 3/2 (December, 1927), p.36.

Many Indians who were revived by the revivals could take a step forward by the work of these early Pentecostal missionaries. All of them were working in association with Indians. There were no much problems between natives and missionaries in the first decade of their work. Struggles began by 1925 to bring the church under the administrative control of natives which caused for division.

2.4.   Emergence of Indigenous Leadership

Missionaries from the West came to India with the Pentecostal message at the beginning of the 20th century. By making use of the natives who were revived by the three great revivals and by the help of Brethren movement, they proclaimed Pentecostal messages. Thus many independent congregations were formed. Since there were no able native leaders, missionaries themselves gave active leadership to the work in Kerala. C. Manasse, A.C. Mathai and Oommen Mammen received baptism in the Holy Spirit and co-operated with the missionaries for the expansion of the work in Kerala. A.C.Mathai (Pandalam) was working in association with Aldivingle in South Travancore and later with Robert F.Cook in Central Travancore, while C.Manasse was working in association with Mary W.Chapman in South Travancore.[54]

2.4.1. Formation of Pentecostal Congregations

By the activists of the missionaries and the natives a few congregations were formed in Central and Southern part of Travancore. Ms. Bouncil and Ms.Aldivingle, the independent missionaries were instrumental in forming different Pentecostal congregations at Paraniyam, Pulugal, Melppuram, Vallarakkavilla, Irennipuram, Plantop and Kulachal in South Travancore.[55] Later, by the influence of Mary W. Chapman,

---

[54] P.D.Johnson, *op.cit.*, p.23.

[55] T.G.Oommen, *IPC yum Anpathu Varshathe Sevana Charithravum* (Malayalam) [IPC and its fifty years service], Mallappally: Mallappally Printers., 1979, p.6.

Aldivingle joined the General Council of the Assemblies of God. By the missionary work of Mrs. Mary W.Chapman churches were also formed at Kuzhithura, Kaithakuzhi, Palliyadi, Mekkod in South Travancore and Pandalam, Kadampanad and Iverkala in Central Travancore.[56] These were the early **Assemblies of God** congregations. Robert F.Cook, who concentrated his work in Central Travancore formed congregations at Thuvayoor, Adoor, Chaliyakkara, Vilakkudy, Punalur, Edamon, Kottarakara, Kumbanad, Mavelikkra and Piravam. His congregations were known as **The Full Gospel Church in Malabar.**[57] K.E.Abraham, a disciple of K.V. Simon and a member of Brethren Church, who learned about baptism in the Holy Spirit from A.C.Mathai, received this experience while praying for it in the house of C. Manasse in South Travancore on 22nd April, 1923. In the following year congregations were formed at Pandalam, Vettiyar, Elanthoor, Mezhuvali, and Cheriyanad, in Central Travancore by his evangelistic activities. He had named these congregations as **South Indian Pentecostal Church of God.**[58]

Robert F.Cook, Mrs.Mary.W.Chapman and K.E.Abraham were the three people involved in the leadership struggle at the first phase of the history of the Pentecostal churches in Kerala. At first there were struggle between Cook and Mrs. Chapman, then between K.E.Abraham and Mrs. Chapman, then with A G and Cook, finally with Cook and K.E.Abraham.

2.4.2. *Struggle between Robert F.Cook and Mrs. Mary W. Chapman*

Cook, who established many churches in the Central Travancore, went to USA in February 1924 for his furlough. Spencer May, an Assemblies of God missionary came to Travancore in 1922 who was residing at Kottarakara, was in

---

[56]A.C.Samuel, *op.cit.,* p.21, 22.

[57] T.M.Varghese and E.V.George, *op.cit.,* p.15.

[58] K.E.Abraham, *IPC Praramba Varshangal* pp.23-33.

charge of Cook's field during his leave. But Mrs.Chapman influenced K.E.Abraham, an able native leader who was working in association with Cook. She sought his help to get a house for rent near Chengannur. Thus in 1924 December Mrs.Chapman and Miss.Aldivingle shifted their residence from Trivandrum to Angadickal in Chengannur. According to K.E.Abraham: "The change of residence from Trivandrum to Chengannur was to extend some help to the people affected by the flood in 1924."[59] But Dora P.Myers interpreted it as an attempt of Mrs.Chapman to bring the congregation of Cook under her control. Spencer E.May understood the plan of Mrs. Chapman, shifted his residence from Kottarakara to Mazhukkeer in Chengannur to protect the work of Cook.[60] Chapman's desire to bring the work of Cook under her control is evident form her attempt to interrupt Cook's return journey. "Since Cook became an affiliated missionary of AG, Mrs.Chapman the official missionary of AG in South India tried to prevent his return journey."[61] Almost a year was delayed for his return and many people had written letters requesting him to come back to India.[62]

In 1925, William M.Faux, secretary of the Foreign Mission Department of the American Assemblies of God visited South India, conducted tarry meetings and Bible classes both in Angadickal and Mazhukeer.[63] During the missionary Tour of William M.Faux to South India people requested him to send a missionary to oversee the work in India. About this William M. Faux writes: "We are then asked to meet a committee of eleven members who literally begged the Foreign Mission Department of the Assemblies of God to send them an

---

[59] K.E.Abraham, *Yesukristhuvinte ... op.cit.,* p.90.

[60] Dora P.Myers, *op.cit.,* p.52.

[61] *Ibid.*

[62] Mammen Philip, *Robert F.Cook* (Malayalam), Vennikkulam: Deepam Book Club, 1992, p.111.

[63] A.C.Samuel, *op.cit.,* p.23.

ordained missionary to oversee the work."[64] William M.Faux, who felt the need of more missionaries in India, reported it to the General Council of the AG. Then the General Council of the AG decided to send Cook back to India and also to accept Blossom Cook, the elder daughter of Cook, as an affiliated missionary. The report in the Pentecostal Evangel reads thus: "Blossom goes out as new missionary. Brother and Sister Cook are returning for another term of service. They will be located at Kottarakara."[65] Mrs. Chapman's attempt to hinder the return of Cook to Travancore was not successful and Cook reached Kottarakkara in 1926 and then moved to Chengannur. As soon as Cook arrived in Travancore Chapman changed her residence from Chengannur to Quilon and then to Mavelikkara.

2.4.3. *Struggle between K.E. Abraham and Mrs. Mary W. Chapman*

K.E.Abraham who formed a few churches in Central Travancore had good relationship with Mrs.Mary W. Chapman and Robert F.Cook. Since Cook was working in Central Travancore they co-operated on many occasions. At the beginning of South India Pentecostal Church, there were no church buildings for worship. Members were very poor and they could not afford to construct a church building. When Cook was away for his furlough, after a long discussion South India Pentecostal Church decided to co-operate with Mary W.Chapman, especially to obtain financial help for the construction of church building.[66] About it K.E.Abraham writes that Mrs. Chapman and Miss.Aldivingle were invited to the meetings held at Mulakkuzha, Punnakkadu, Kidangannoor, Poovanmala and Chethakkal. Mrs.Chapman has agreed to give money to construct a hall at Chethakkal in

---

[64] William M.Faux, "Missionary Tour", Gary.B.McGee(ed.), *Selected Documents on the Early History of the Assemblies of God in India*, Springfield: Assemblies of God, 1991, p.17.

[65] "Report", *Pentecostal Evangel* (August, 1926), p.19.

[66] Saju, *op.cit.*, pp.74, 75.

Ranny, in the ten cent plot obtained as a gift to the church from Bro. Kutty of Maliakkamannil.[67] But when they discussed for the registration of the land Mrs. Chapman informed that the money should be provided only if the land is registered in the name of the Secretary of the General Council of the Assemblies of God in America. It was difficult for K.E.Abraham and his associates to agree to this point. They decided that though the money is not obtained from the missionary, the land should be registered only in the name of the local church.[68] A similar event which took place among the Brethrens might have influenced them to take this decision.[69] Besides P.E.Mammen, who belongs to Syrian Brethren Group, published many tracts emphasizing the independence of local churches from foreign domination with the scriptural evidences. K.E.Abraham, formerly a member of the Brethren group had read these tracts and it influenced him to move forward to an independent Pentecostal Church without any foreign domination.[70] Thus South India Pentecostal Church of God in its struggle for existence had to break its relation with Mary Chapman. The decision of the South India Pentecostal Church to register the land in the name of local church was the first step taken towards the establishment of independent Pentecostal Church in Kerala.

2.4.4. *Struggle between Assemblies of God Missionaries and Native Leaders*

2.4.4.1. *Malankara Pentecostal Church of God*

Most of the people, attracted to the Pentecostal churches in the period between 1923 to 1925, were from the Brethren churches.[71] K.V.Simon a well-known scholar and writer of

---

[67] K.E.Abraham, *Yesukristhuvinte... op.cit.,* pp.142, 143.

[68] *Ibid.*

[69] See above [Brethren Movement (1.3)], pp.14 &15.

[70] K.E.Abraham, *Yesukristhuvinte... op.cit.,* p.80.

[71] Saju, *Nallavanum Viswasthanumaya Dasan* (Malayalam) [Good and Faithful Servant], Kottayam: Goodnews Publications, 1995, p.36.

Brethren Group openly fought against Pentecostalism, especially its teaching of speaking in tongues. Arattupuzha Brethren convention of 1926 was held at the second week of February. On Saturday, 13th February K.V.Simon preached on the subject "Scripture and other tongues" and he severely criticized the practice of speaking in tongues. K.C.Oommen, K.C.Cherian, K.E.Abraham and A.C.Samuel decided to conduct a convention from February 18 to 21 at the same place uniting all Pentecostal churches in Central Travancore, to answer the questions raised by K.V.Simon against Pentecostal teaching on speaking in tongues. A.R.Thankayya Athisayam attended both of these meetings was convinced of Pentecostal teachings, testified it on Sunday, 21st February.[72] This convention was very successful and Pentecostal teachings deep-rooted in Travancore and many adopted Pentecostal faith.

Inspired by the united convention, K.C.Oommen longed for the union of all Pentecostal churches. K.C.Oommen and A.C.Samuel who were formerly the members of Syrian Brethren which stood for the independence of native churches, wrote to Cook about the need of union with K.E.Abraham and their groups. Since Cook agreed to develop an independent church without having any foreign dominion, K.E.Abraham and his group decided to join together to form 'Malankara Pentecostal Church of God'. The General Body of the church was held at Mazhukeer on 6th October, 1926 that formed an eleven member executive committee, in which, Cook and K.E.Abraham were president and vice-president respectively.[73] At the time of union South India Pentecostal Church had 12 churches.[74]

---

[72] K.E.Abraham, *Yesukristhuvinte... op.cit.,* pp.130,131.

[73] K.E.Abraham, *IPC Praramba Varshangal,* pp.86, 87.

[74] K.E.Abraham, "Indian Pentecosthu Swathanthra Sabhakal" (Malayalam) [Independent Indian Pentecostal Churches], *Zion Kahalam,* 2/7 (July, 1938), p.181.

Cook who agreed to administer the church independently, gave a little financial help to the native workers. About it K.E.Abraham writes, "Robert F.Cook was giving a regular financial help every month to all the ministers including me".[75] People like K.M.Zakariah thought that the union with the churches of Cook will hinder the independence of the local churches and did not participate in the union.

Even though Cook and his work were independent, he was affiliated to the General Council of AG and was working in relation to it since 1919. Cook's name is found 10th in the list of the Directory of the Missionaries to India holding certificates of appointment from the Assemblies of God published in 1922.[76] It was just for a sponsorship after the First World War.[77] But his affiliation to the General Council of the AG could obtain enough money to the work in Travancore and the influence of K.E.Abraham could provide co-workers. All these helped to the growth of Pentecostal churches in Kerala. Thus the union of these two different Pentecostal groups as one organization strengthened the Pentecostal work and many churches were established in the following years.[78]

2.4.4.2. *Poowathur Revival – 1929*

One of the important events happened during this period was the revival at Poowathur, which spread all around Travancore. It was not a revival imported by the foreign agents but was purely indigenous in its origin. As in the case of other revivals in the 19th century, Poowathur revival also happened by the ministry of a person from Tamil Nadu, called A.R.Thankayya Athisayam.

---

[75] K.E.Abraham, *Yesukristhuvinte...* , p.180.

[76] Gary B.McGee (ed.), *Selected Documents...* , p.12.

[77] Sunny P.Samuel (ed.), *Church of God (Full Gospel) In India Kerala State Convention Souvenir*, Mulakkuzha: State Council, 1996, p.6.

[78] K.E.Abraham, *Yesukristhuvinte....*, p.145.

Poowathur revival was started in the middle of July 1929.[79] A.R.T.Athisayam, who was convinced of the Pentecostal teachings, received baptism in the Holy Spirit on 5th May 1929.[80] When Poowathur independent Brethren Church [Swatanthra Viyojithar] heard about the new experience of Thankayya Athiysayam, they invited him to Poowathur to conduct tarry meetings and he arrived Poowathur in the beginning of July 1929. Within two weeks many received baptism in the Holy Spirit.[81] K.P.Philip, the headmaster of Keezhillam Marthoma English School remarks the revival in following words: "who will not exclaim when they hear the interpretation of the Greek and English tongues that has spoken by the poor people who do not know Malayalam well".[82] T.M.Varghese, who gave active leadership to the Pentecostal churches in Kerala, also received baptism in the Holy Spirit in August 1929 at Zion Bible School during the time of Poowathur Revival.[83]

Almost all leaders of the Pentecostal churches had experienced the blessings of Poowathur revival. Since the revival happened at the formative period of Pentecostal churches it influenced greatly to the growth of Pentecostal churches in Kerala, that can be compared with the revival in

---

[79] K.P.Philip, "Parisudhalma Snanasakshiangal" (Malayalam) [Testimony of baptism in the Holy Spirit], *Suvisesha Prabhashakan* 3/2. (August-September, 1929), p.19.

[80] Letter Addressed to P.T.Mathew, Podimala, Poowattur, by A.R.Thankayya Athisayam of 14th May, 1929 cited in *Suvisesha Prabhashakan*, 2/10 & 11 (May-June, 1929), pp.258,259.

[81] K.E.Abraham, "Oru Unarvinte Aarambam" (Malayalam) [Begginning of a revival], *Suvisesha Prabhashakan*, Vol.II, No.12 (July, 1929), p.296.

[82] K.P.Philip, *op.cit.*, p.20

[83] T.M.Varghese, "Parisudhalma Snana Sakshiangal" (Malayalam) [Testimony of baptism in the Holy Spirit], *Suvisesha Prabhashakan*, 3/1& 2 (August-September, 1929), p. 28.

Wales.[84] But the Poowathur revival did not become as famous as of Wales or Los Angeles, because it occurred in the East, not in the West. Usual tendency of western dominance is also found in the case of revival and Pentecostalism.

2.4.4.3. *South India and Ceylon District Council of Assemblies of God*

During this period the number of churches of Assemblies of God and their missionary force increased in Kerala. In order to organize the missionary work in South India and Ceylon, the General Council of the Assemblies of God decided to form South India and Ceylon District Council and it was formed in 1929. Report in the 'Pentecostal Evangel' read thus: "...request was made from the home office to organize a District Council for South India and Ceylon."[85]

Missionaries were the members of the Council. Walter Clifford was elected as the superintendent in 1929 at the formation of South India and Ceylon District Council and it was believed to be a plot against Cook by other missionaries then working in South India.[86]

Natives who co-operated with Cook were also dissatisfied with the policy of the General Council for restricting their independence by forming a Council. K.E.Abraham writes: "It has grieved the natives that the council had made some restrictions and control over the missionary work in South India which would lead to the control of foreign missionaries rather than guidance of the spirit."[87]

---

[84] Sunny P.Samuel, *Pastor A.R.T. Athisayam* (Malayalam), Mulakkuzha: Bethestha Books, 1995, pp.15, 83.

[85] "Report", *Pentecostal Evangel,* (July 6, 1929), p.7.

[86] Letter addressed to Gary B.Mc.Gee, A.G.Theological Seminary, Springfield, from George and Mariam Cook on 19th September, 1985.

[87] K.E.Abraham, "Njangalude Naveena Padhathi" (Malayalam) [Our New Plan], *Suvisesha Prabhashakan,* 2/12 (July, 1929), p.289.

The revival at Mt.Zion Bible School in 1929 enlarged the missionary vision of Cook to trust in God rather than to depend upon foreign mission body. Cook says that it is not good for an evangelist or a pastor to expect a monthly payment for their ministry, but to trust in God for every needs.[88]

Miss. Mildred Ginn, who was working in Kerala for about 40 years, rightly pointed out the reasons for the breach of his relation with AG in the following words:

> "...Cook was disappointed with the position he had in the missionary fellowship and with pressure also from his workers headed by K.E.Abraham who desired to be independent of foreign organization".[89]

Within a few years of his contact Cook could understand the ability, knowledge and maturity of Christians in Travancore to progress independently without having any relation to foreign mission. So he decided to severe his relations with AG to work independently as in the early days of his work(1913-19). Though Cook broke his relation with AG he believed that there should be a council to administer the church. This council should be constituted by the representatives from the churches in India and have easy access to deal the matters of the church.[90]

---

[88] Robert F.Cook, "Sabhakariyam" (Malayalam) [Church Matter], *Suvisesha Prabhashakan*, 3/1 & 2 (August-September, 1929), 6. In Half a century of Divine Leadings... Cook wrote, "During the revival of 1929, the Lord Spoke to me quit definitely that we should sever ourselves from all which hindered us from an implicit walk of faith with Him"- p.201.

[89] Letter addressed to Benjamin Prasad Shinde by Miss.Mildred Ginn on 28th February, 1974.

[90] R.F.Cook "Editorial – Alochana Sabha" (Malayalam) [Church Councils], *Suvisesha Prabhashakan*, 3/4 (November, 1929).

The separation of Cook and other native leaders who were co-operating with the AG till 1929, was a great blow to the work of AG in Kerala, but was an important step taken by the native leaders to the growth of the church in India. This event helped to develop an Indian leadership for the Pentecostal churches in Kerala.

2.4.5. *Struggle between Robert F. Cook and Native Leaders*

Rama Paul, born in 1881 as a son of a Hindu priest, became a CMS minister in 1921, received baptism in the Holy Spirit in 1924, adopted 'faith-living', established many churches known as Ceylon Pentecostal Mission.[91] Kochukunju Vaidyer, a leader of the Viyojitha group (Brethren), baptized by K.E. Abraham, visited Ceylon in 1928, invited Paul to conduct tarry meetings at Aaramada. Many of the members of the Viyojitha group received baptism in the Holy Spirit in those meetings and Viyojitha Church at Aaramada became Pentecostal.[92]

This church was purely an indigenous one in its existence and propagation of the gospel. Four conventions were held in the year 1929 spending about 500 rupees collected from the local church. 'Suvisesha Prabhashakan' gives a report about convention says: "Aaramada Church originated and exists without having any relation to foreign mission. The minister and his associates in the church are able to train people to continue the work without any foreign support."[93] Teaching of the independence of local church in Viyojitha group, in which Kochukunju Vaidyar was a member, and the influence of Paul might have been there behind the decision to exist without having any relation to foreign mission.

---

[91] Daniel Ayroor, *op.cit.*, pp 64, 65.

[92] Pastor Paul, *Jeevacharithra Samgraham* (Malayalam) [A biography of Pastor Paul], Trivandrum: Pentecostal Press Trust, 1994, pp.117,118.

[93] "Thekken Thiruvanthamkur Convention" (Malayalam) [South Travancore Convention], *Suvisesha Prabhashakan*, 2/8 & 9(March-April, 1929), p. 228.

P.M. Samuel an evangelist of Viyojitha Church founded 17 churches, visited Ceylon in 1929, received baptism in the Holy Spirit in the meetings of Ceylon Pentecostal Mission conducted by Paul on 20th September 1929.[94] When he returned to Keekkozhoor in Kerala he propagated the Pentecostal teaching. Itty Mathai of Kalayapuram also accepted Pentecostal teaching by the ministry of Paul in this period, while he was in Ceylon for the business.[95] On his return Itty Mathai also gave active leadership to the Pentecostal churches in Kerala.

Robert F. Cook and K.E. Abraham shared the pulpit along with pastor Paul of Ceylon in the convention of Aaramada Church in South Travancore, invited Paul to preach in the General Convention of 'Malankara Pentecostal Church of God' in 1930, held at central Travancore from January 13 to 19. Paul was also the main preacher in the convention held at Keekozhoor and Ranny in the same year from January 23 to 26 and from January 29 to February 2 respectively. Paul's testimony challenged most of the people who attended in those conventions.[96] Most of the ministers of the Malankara Pentecostal Church of God including K. E. Abraham, were influenced by the teaching of Paul on 'faith-living' as in the days of Apostles. The regular support they receive from Cook is thought as against 'faith-living', practiced in the apostolic days. They also thought that the independence of the local churches will not be protected in the 'Malankara Pentecostal Church of God' led by R.F.Cook. Thus in January 1930, K.E.Abraham and his co-workers decided to separate from Cook and continue their work in the former name 'South India Pentecostal Church of God'.[97]

---

[94] P.M.Samuel, "Parisudhalma Snana Sakshiam" (Malayalam) [Testimony of the baptism in the Holy Spirit], *Suvisesha Prabhashakan*, Vol. III, No.3 (October, 1929), p. 70.

[95] Saju, *Kerala Pentecosthu Charithram, op.cit.,* p.206.

[96] K.E.Abraham *Yesukristhuvinte... op.cit.,* p.179.

[97] Saju, *Daivathinte Manushyan* (Malayalam) [Man of God], Kuriannoor: Margam Books, 1989, pp.41, 42.

It is clear that teaching on 'faith-living' at the 1930 General convention influenced them to separate from Cook. Cook writes: "Spirit of disunity began to work after the convention".[98] One of the major complaints of K.E.Abraham against Cook were found in the following words:

> "Though a committee consisting eleven members was formed when the union of churches took place; the affairs of the church were carried on without the consent of the committee. Pastor Cook, who was firm in adopting his policy could not accept our views of having freedom for local churches."[99]

Cook arranged the financial support from the Highway Mission Tabernacle in Philadelphia, Pennsylvania from the time he left the AG,[100] was distributed to the ministers regularly and asked to send a report of their work. K.E.Abraham thought it as against 'faith-living' as revealed in the New Testament. Habel.G.Varghese, his biographer says that he was not at all an anti-missionary, but was only against 'the master-attitude' of the missionaries.[101] The spirit of nationalism that was prevalent in Kerala during the period inspired K.E.Abraham to separate from Cook, a foreigner, to build up a native church independent from foreign mission body.[102] Though the division was healed by the mediators from Kumbanadu, it did not last long because of the non-co-operation of the natives who adopted their former name 'South India

---

[98] R.F.Cook, "Pathradhipa Lekhanam" (Malayalam) [Editorial], *Suvisesha Prabhashakan* 3/8 (March, 1930), p.205.

[99] K.E.Abraham, "The Indian Pentecostal Church of God" *IPC Jubliee Souvenir* (1924-1974), Kumbanad: IPC, 1974, appendix ii.

[100] Letter addressed to Gary, B.McGee, from George and Mariam Cook, on 19th September, 1985.

[101] Habel.G.Varghese, K.E.Abraham: *An Apostle From Modern India*, Kadambanad: The Christian Literature Service of India, 1974, p.50.

[102] M.A.Thomas, *An Outline History of Christian Churches and Denominations in Kerala*, Trivandrum: M.A.Thomas, 1977, p.157.

Pentecostal Church of God' to continue their work.[103] When a group headed by K.E.Abraham separated from Cook, Cook called a general body of the Full Gospel Church of Malabar on 24th May at Mount Zion, Mulakuzha in which more than 40 members were present. R.F.Cook as the President and T. M.Varghese as Secretary, a nine member administrative council was formed.[104] Membership in the Administrative Council shows that it was constituted by the natives. Though Cook was a foreigner, his work was independent from the control of foreign mission body from 1929 to 1936.

The Native leaders and missionaries who co-operated in their work till the end of 1920's divided into three groups. Thus in the beginning of 1930 there were three different Pentecostal churches in the organized form, along with many other independent groups. The work of Assemblies of God in Kerala was administered by foreign missionaries while South India Pentecostal Church of God and Full Gospel Church in Malabar were administered by the natives. Though Cook the President of Full Gospel Church in Malabar, was a foreigner, all the others in the nine member administrative committee were natives. Thus the Pentecostal work in Kerala began in 1909 by the foreign missionaries who came under the administration of the natives by the beginning of 1930's.

---

[103] R.F.Cook, "Pathradihipa Lekhanam" (Malayalam) [Editorial], *Suvisesha Prabhashakan*, 3/8 (March, 1930), p.205.

[104] T.M.Varghese, "A Forward Move" (Malayalam) *Suvisesha Prabhashakan*, 3/9 & 10 (April-May, 1930), p.247.

CHAPTER III

Progress of the Church Under Indigenous Leadership

As we have seen, at the beginning of 1930's there were three major denominations among the Pentecostals existing independently. At first, two of them viz. South Indian Pentecostal Church of God and Full Gospel Church in Malabar were administered by the natives without having any control from the mission body; and AG Work as part of the General Council of the Assemblies of God in USA. By implementing the indigenous policy of the General Council of the Assemblies of God, it had come under the administrative control of natives in 1947, while Full Gospel Church in Malabar came under the administrative control of Church of God, Cleveland, Tennesse, USA, in 1936. In 1953, P.J.Thomas, an ordained minister of Indian Pentecostal Church of God organized an independent work at the wake of split in Indian Pentecostal Church, which is also in progress under native leadership. There are also many other independent organizations like Church of God, Kalayapuram, New India Church of God, New India Bible Church, etc., under native leadership without having any relation with foreign body. But here we deal only these four major Pentecostal Churches namely, Indian Pentecostal Church of God, Assemblies of God, Sharon Fellowship Church and Church of God (Full Gospel) in India.

3.1. Indian Pentecostal Church of God

Many of the native leaders influenced by the teaching of Paul, a preacher of the General convention of 1930, on 'faith-living', separated from R.F.Cook and began to work independently, taking their former name, South India Pentecostal Church. Kochukunju Vaidyar of Aaramada, and P.M.Samuel received 'baptism in the Holy Spirit' by the ministry of Paul in Ceylon in 1928, joined with South India Pentecostal Church along with their churches, because Pastor Paul was working in co-operation with it during the early period. Some independent churches also joined with South Indian Pentecostal Church when it has become independent. About it K.E.Abraham himself says: "When we started to work independently, Pastor P.M.Samuel and Kouchukunju Vaidyar along with their churches and many of you joined us in the ministry of the Lord".[1] P.M.Samuel had 17 churches at the time he joined with South Indian Pentecostal Church and established 15 more churches at Tamil Nadu within few months of his work in 1930.[2] Thus thirty two churches out of fifty,[3] in 1936, were established by P.M.Samuel. He also established many churches in Andhra Pradesh and the church made rapid progress in establishing churches beyond the region of Kerala. The workers, on faith, went to Tamil Nadu, Andhra Pradesh, Karnataka and Northern part of India and established many churches. During this period there were many natives who desired to exist independently. C.V.Tharappan gives a list of 25 places in Kerala, in his book published in 1926, where there were independent churches progressing without missionary control.[4] Since Abraham learned that most people desired to

---

[1] K.E.Abraham, "Indian Pentecosthu Swathanthra Sabhakal" (Malayalam), [Independent Indian Pentecostal Church], *Zion Kahalam* [Zion Trumphet] 2/7 (July, 1938): p.182.

[2] Saju, Keralathile Pentecosthu Sabhakalude Aarambavum Valarchayum (Malayalam) [Origin and growth of Pentecostal Churches in Kerala], *Goodnews* 16/10 (March 8, 1993): pp.19, 20.

[3] T.G.Oommen, *I.P.C.yum Anpathu Varshathe Sevana Charithravum* (Malayalam) [I.P.C. and History of fifty years Ministry], Mallappally: The Mallappally Printers, 1979, p.17.

[4] C.V.Tharappan, *Kristhiya Sabha Charithram* (Malayalam) [History of Christian Church], 2nd ed., Kunnamkulam: K.O.Cheru, 1976, p.230.

exist independently from the foreign missionary control he tried to organize them by promising the independence of local church and was successful in his attempt.

There was no administrative council during the early period of the church. In June 1933 a minister's council was formed constituting twelve pastors, in which P.M.Samuel was elected as President.[5] Since the church spread outside South India, the Council meeting held on 9th April, 1934 decided to change the name as **'Indian Pentecostal Church of God'** (IPC) and was registered at Elloor (Andhra) in British India on 9th December, 1935.[6] According to T.G.Oommen one of the four main purposes behind the formulation of Indian Pentecostal Church of God is to exist and work independently without joining any foreign missionary organization and be self-reliant.[7] K.E.Abraham was elected as the president of IPC in 1936 and continued till his death in 1974. Abraham had the nature to appreciate and give fellowship to able persons and it helped in the progress of the work.[8] Thus many co-workers rose up to shoulder the responsibilities of the work, stood as a team with K.E.Abraham to propagate the Pentecostal teachings all over India.

3.1.1. Teachings on the Independence of the Local Church

The vision of an independent Pentecostal Church, that progress in India, is found in the teachings and writings of the early leaders. The early leaders of the Indian Pentecostal Church gave emphasis for the independence of the local church. In

---

[5] K.E.Abraham, *Yesukristhuvinte Eliya Dasan Athava Pastor K.E.Abraham* (Malayalam) [Humble Servant of Jesus Christ: The autobiography of Pastor K.E.Abraham], 2nd ed., Kumbanand: K.E.Abraham Foundations, 1983, p.244.

[6] K.E.Abraham, *IPC Praramba Varshangal* (Malayalam) [the early years of IPC], 2nd ed., Kumbanand: K.E.Abraham Foundations, 1986, p.112.

[7] T.G.Oommen, *IPC yum Anpathu Varshathe Sevana Charithravum*, p.177.

[8] K.E.Abraham, *Yesukristhuvinte........, op. cit.*, p.407.

the writings of K.C.Cherian, K.E.Abraham, and T.G.Oommen we find emphasis on the independence of local church. According to them each congregation is free and independent and the attempt to govern and control by a foreign mission body is unbiblical. When K.C.Cherian comments on the New Testament pattern of 'independence of local church, he says, "Though all the ministers in Apostolic period had gone out from Jerusalem Church and established many churches, neither the Jerusalem Church, nor the ministers argued for the control over those churches".[9] Jerusalem church did not argue for control over churches in Samaria, and Antioch. Antiochean church also did not claim authority over the churches that were established by Paul and Barnabans. Churches established in Asia and Europe by the missionary journey of Paul and Silas were also progressed independently. Therefore the biblical pattern of the church is stated as independent, and at the same time co-operating each other in Christian love.

There is no evidence in the New Testament to say that the churches which gave financial help at the time of need, have authority over the churches that received the help. The help given was out of concern for the fellow brethren, not to govern them. Therefore local pastor serve the needs of church and the ministry of Apostles is not given to govern but to co-operate in the ministry.[10] K.E. Abraham had the opinion that the foreign missionaries who pay regularly to the Indian ministers to work for their mission organization is not according to the New Testament pattern. A minister has to trust in God for every need and God will provide him. The churches which we find in the scripture were independent

---

[9] K.C.Cherian, *"Sthalam Sabhakalude Swathanthriam"* (Malayalam) [Independence of the local churches], Zion Kahalam [Zion Trumphet] 1/11 (November 1937): p.291.

[10] *Ibid.,* pp.291-293.

and we can follow only such examples.[11] According to T.G.Oommen: "All local churches should be independent and ministered by the pastor and should be helped by the ministry of the Apostles. There should not be any authority over an elder or an Apostle".[12]

K.C.Cherian had the opinion that all the properties of the church should be registered in the name of local church, not in the name of any other person outside the church. The help that is given for the church from any source should be for the church, i.e., church should be given power and authority to utilize it, not the donor. The attempt of missionaries to control the church is interpreted as satanic and contemptuous and not according to the biblical teaching, but against the example of early church.[13] One of the main reasons that missionaries says against transferring the power and responsibilities to the natives is that they are not educated and capable to become leaders. But K.C.Cherian says if Indian politics could contribute leaders from the country, why not there are leaders to minister the church? It is because of the wrong impression that Indians themselves have given to the missionaries.[14] Therefore missionaries who implement indigenous principles in Western countries were not willing to apply it in India. According to K.E.Abraham: "…the work in India will not be successful until it should apply indigenous methods".[15] For the progress of the work in India, early leaders of the Indian Pentecostal Church of God suggested that the missionaries should come to the level of serving as co-workers with natives

---

[11] K.E.Abraham, "Suvisesha Parisramam Indiayil Vijaya-pradhamakunnathe Enganne?" (Malayalam) [How can the evangelization in India be victorious], *Zion Kahalam.* 2/2 & 3 (February-March, 1938): pp.68-71.

[12] T.G.Oommen, Atmakatha (Malayalam) [Autobiography], Kuwait: Kuwait I.P.C., 1984, p.73.

[13] K.C.Cherian, "Sthalam Sabakalude…. 1/12 (December, 1937): p.315.

[14] *Ibid.*

[15] K.E.Abraham, "Suvisesha Parisramam….." *op.cit.,* p.71.

by giving independence to the Indian Church with full authority and responsibilities to the natives.[16]

3.1.2. Factors that Influenced the Early Leaders

The early leaders got the vision of an independent Indian Church mainly from the teaching of the New Testament. Since Pentecostals seeks evidences from scripture for everything, they found independence of local church is according to the biblical pattern. Secondly, most of the early Pentecostals were coming from the Brethren background which teach and believe in the independence of local church as the pattern of the New Testament church. Thirdly, they were influenced by the tracts published by P.E.Mammen, a leader of Syrian Brethrens which emphasized the native leadership, quoting biblical evidences to the independence of local church.[17] Fourthly, the teaching of Paul of Cylon, on 'faith-living' as in the days of Apostles influenced many natives. Fifthly, the success of many traditional churches struggled for independence of the church from missionary control gave encouragement to the attempt.[18] Sixthly, the knowledge obtained from prophetical books, that India will be independent gave impetus to work for an independent church. Seventhly, struggle for Indian independence was so accute that they also must take a stand which help the church to progress in independent India.

3.1.3. Indian Pentecostal Church of God and its Foreign
Connection

While Indian Pentecostal Church was progressing under native leadership, without having any financial assistance from abroad, Karl Swan, a missionary from Swedish Pentecostal

---

[16] K.C.Cherian, *op.cit.,* p.316.

[17] K.E.Abraham, *Yesukristhuvinte Eliya Dassan......* *op.cit.,* p.316.

[18] V.J.Varghese, "Chinthavishayam" (Malayalam) [theme of thought], Zion Kahalam [Zion Trumphet] 1/11 (November, 1937), cover page 2.

Church, who heard about the independent Pentecostal work in Kerala, attended a special meeting held from August 14 to 20 in 1935. At his return, Levi Pethrus, the leader of the Swedish Pentecostal Church, sent letters inviting K.E.Abraham and K.C.Cherian to preach in the convention held in Sweden from June 15-21, 1936. The Indian brothers who set out to the first Swedish journey in April 1936 returned in 1938.[19] By the first visit, they could own properties at not less than forty places. K.E.Abraham himself wrote about the financial help obtained from the Swedish Church as follows:

> "The Brothers from Swedish Church are ready to support us to progress in our work to be independent from foreign mission body by giving financial assistance to buy cemeteries and church buildings. They were not giving any help to any of the ministers including Cherian and I."[20]

K.E.Abraham who had the vision of an Indian Church did not arrange any financial assistance to ministers which make them lazy. But he requested the churches to support their pastors, and encouraged the ministers to trust in God for their needs, rather than looking to any of the missionary organizations. His emphasis on this matter appeared in his letter written from Sweden thus: The ministers are not getting any financial help from Sweden. It is the duty of the local church to meet the needs of their pastors, not of the Swedish Church. To the progress of the church it is good to stand on our own legs.[21] One noteworthy thing was that Swedish Church did not demand any report for the financial assistance. They did not try to bring the Indian Church under their control. Mar Aprem comments about the

---

[19] K.E.Abraham, *Yesukristuvinte*......, pp.251, 260-61.

[20] K.E.Abraham, *"Suvisesha Parisramam......."* *op.cit.,* p.69.

[21] Letter addressed to the IPC Ministers, Kumbanad, by K.E.Abraham, dated August 9th, 1937 cited in *Zion Kahalam* [Zion Trumphet], 1/9 (September, 1937): p.244.

Swedish relation thus: "Pastor K. E. Abraham once again joined with the foreign bodies, without foreign domination."[22]

When T.G.Oommen writes about the first period of the history of IPC, that is from 1930-1938, says that all churches were self supported, self propagated and independent. They had brotherly concern, love and equality. There was no custom of giving report about their work and most of the gatherings were held in private houses.[23] But during the second period (i.e. from 1938-1953), with the financial assistance obtained from Sweden IPC owned properties at many places and built churches. Though the financial assistance obtained from Sweden helped to the expansion of Indian Pentecostal Church of God, there are people who held the view that, it became a cause for disunity and internal strife.[24] Therefore the foreign money became impairment rather a blessing to the Pentecostal Churches in Kerala.

3.1.4. Opposition from the Missionaries

The natives, who took an independent stand, were opposed by the missionaries. The foreign missionaries in India tried to prevent the journey of K.E.Abraham and K.C.Cherian to Sweden and United States. About it K.E.Abraham writes: "We found letters in the hands of every leaders of the churches which we had visited requesting them not to receive us."[25] But in Sweden there were many Independent Pentecostal Churches which progress without the help from the foreign mission board and those churches appreciated the step taken by the natives. Levi Pethrus, a Swedish Pentecostal leader

---

[22] Mar Aprem, *Indian Christian Directory*, Bangalore: Bangalore Parish Church of the East, 1984, p.129.

[23] T.G.Oommen, *IPCyum.....* *op.cit.,* p.22.

[24] Saju, "Keralathile Pentecosthu Sabhakalude Arambavum Valarchayum", *Goodnews* 26/10 (March 8, 1993):p.26.

[25] Letter addressed to the IPC Ministers, Kumbanad by K.E.Abraham, dated August 9th,1937 cited in *Zion Kahalam* [Zion Trumphet], 1/9 (September, 1937): p.242.

wrote in Evangel Herald thus: "Missionaries oppose the natives because the natives do not like to continue under the control of missionaries, who consider them as children or servants and demand obedience without questioning."[26] In his opinion it is wise and more Christian for the missionaries to handover the power and responsibilities to the natives than to be carried out by the missionaries. The Swedish Pentecostals appreciated the leadership qualities, eloquency in preaching and knowledge in scripture of the Indian Brothers.[27]

3.1.5. Church Administration

When the number of churches were increased, for the convenience of administration and for the monthly fellowship of churches, it was divided into many centres in 1940.[28] A centre pastor was appointed to each centre. It was also divided into different states on the regional basis such as IPC Northern region, Andhra Pradesh, Karnataka, Tamil Nadu and Kerala.[29] Concerning the administration of the church K.E.Abraham had the opinion that as the local church is administered by the Pastor, General Council should be governed by the Apostles, representing all the regions.[30] Indian Pentecostal Church of God revised its by-laws in 1979 and according to it laymen also got representation in the General and Central Councils. Regional representation was also given to the General Council. Thus the division into different regions and representation on the regional basis helped the growth of the organization. In 1971, Kerala State Council of Indian

---

[26] Levi Pethrus, "Indian Brothers" *Evangel Herald* (July 9, 1937) cited in *Zion Kahalam Yathavasara Lekha*, No.4, (April, 1937): p.23.

[27] *Ibid.*, p.25.

[28] T.G.Oommen IPC yum........, *op.cit.*, p.29.

[29] Daniel Ayroor, *Keralathile Pentecosthu Sabhakal* (Malayalam) [Pentecostal Churches in Kerala] 2nd ed., Mavelikkara: Beer Sheba Bible College, 1986, p.63.

[30] K.E.Abraham, "Sthalam Sabhakalude Swathanthriam" (Malayalam) [Independence of local church] *Zion Kahalam* [Zion Trumphet] Vol.XI, No.5 (May, 1952): p.101.

Pentecostal Church of God was formed, in which representation was given to both ministers and laymen. Women were not elected to the church councils. Indian Pentecostal Church of God, Kerala State is administered by both Presbytery constituted by ministers and State Council.

Indian Pentecostal Church of God was founded in 1923, registered at Elloor in 1935, marked a tremendous growth in India under efficient native leadership. According to K.V.Daniel, the independence of the local churches, availability of the committed ministers and the freedom of the ministers to work independently, contributed to the tremendous growth of the Indian Pentecostal Church of God in Kerala.[31] Efficient leadership of K.E.Abraham at the formative and early period of Indian Pentecostal Church of God also helped to its growth. About it P. D. Johnson, the Assemblies of God superintendent comments: "The secret behind the success of Indian Pentecostal Church of God is the efficient leadership of K.E.Abraham.[32]

One of the important things we notice in the history of the IPC is that the independence of Indian Church from the foreign mission body helped the natives to take the responsibility of the propagation and maintenances of the church by themselves. The financial assistance obtained from other sources was used for earning property and establishing institutions. The financial assistance was not considered as the main source or regular income but the emphasis was given to the ministers to meet their needs from the churches they minister. It helped the natives to be trained to meet the needs by themselves. At present most of the churches are self reliant in their needs and also contribute to the outstation. Thus the

---

[31] Daniel Ayroor, *op.cit.*, p.63.

[32] P.D.Johnson, "K.E.Abraham Mahathwathil" (Malayalam) [K.E.Abraham in glory] Assemblies of God Doothan [Assemblies of God Messenger], 2/3, (December, 1974): p.5.

church under native leadership progress towards self sufficiency. Now the church is striving towards the formation of indigenous church in all its respects. In the struggle for the achievement of indigenous church, it could achieve self-government and self-propagation. It progressed much in the matters of self-support too.[33]

3.1.6. Hebron Bible College

K.E.Abraham, formerly a teacher of Mount Zion Bible Training Institute, started a Bible class at Kumbanad in 1930, came to be known as Hebron Bible College. This school serves as the backbone of the Indian Pentecostal Church of God.[34] The classes were held for two and half months every year from June to August. The school was run without any financial help from any foreign countries till 1950, and teachers were not paid. But from 1951 onwards the teachers were paid by the financial assistance obtained from Congregational Holiness Church.[35] Those who had trained in this school were greatly used for the expansion of IPC. About 80% of IPC pastors were from Hebron Bible College. With a vision to go to other states as missionaries, preaching practice was held in English and P.T.Chacko was in charge of that.[36]

Apart from Hebron Bible College under the auspicies of IPC, there are many Bible Schools run by the pastors of IPC at different places. All these schools helped many to be

---

[33] Special offerings are collected in the first week of June, September, November, December from every local churches of IPC to the needs of Youth activities, Mission work, Charitable work, and Evangelistic activities respectively.

[34] K.E.Abraham, "The Indian Pentecostal Church of God." *The IPC Jubliee Souvenir 1924-1974*, Kumbanad: Hebron Printing Press, 1974, p.22.

[35] T.G.Oommen, IPC yum...... *op.cit.*, p.36.

[36] Hebron Bible College (Mal.) *Zion Kahalam* [Zion Trumphet], 2/8 (August, 1938): p.214.

prepared for the ministry and expansion of the church. In 1995 it was decided to run Hebron Bible College under the direct control of State Council. A post-graduate course started in the same year for the candidates who had successfully completed their course in other Bible Training Centres. The duration of this course is one year and those who complete this course will be appointed as pastors in IPC.[37] Twenty students graduated from here in the year 1995 and sixty were in the role in 1996. The needs of the institution are met by the fund collected from the natives. Offering of one Sunday is set apart to meet the needs of the college[38] and thus the institution is run purely by Indian money.

The church in its struggle for indigenous leadership was successful and its effect was far-reaching. Indian Pentecostal Church of God, as church formed and developed by the Indian leadership grew more than any other organization run by foreign missionaries or later transferred from missionaries to the Indian leadership. It challenged the leaders to develop a consciousness among the members to collect the needed fund to run institutions and charitable works.

3.2.   Sharon Fellowship Church

Sharon fellowship church is one of the most important Pentecostal Churches which developed under native leadership. Even though it was founded only in the 1950's it marked tremendous growth. In the field of theological education its contributions are much praiseworthy.

3.2.1. *Formation of Sharon Fellowship Church*

P.J.Thomas, the son of P.V.John an ordained minister of IPC was invited to Tiruvalla by Pastor J.Varghese and P.K.Chacko

---

[37] Sabu Samuel, "Hebron Bible College" (Malayalam), *Malabar Gospel Messenger*, 5/16 (April 16, 1995): p.8.

[38] Varghese Mathai, "Hebron Bible Collegil Classukal Arambichu" (Malayalam) [Classes began in Hebron Bible College], *Malabar Gospel Messenger*, 6/20 (May 20, 1996): p.8.

to convene a revival meeting. Thus co-operating with his friends Pr.T.G.Oommen, Pr.C.K.Daniel, Pr.P.J.Thomas conducted a revival meeting at Tiruvalla in 1952.[39] After the meeting, P.J.Thomas, guided by the Holy Spirit to start a Bible School, bought a building in the centre of Tiruvalla Town and started Sharon Bible Institute in May 1953. Pastors T.G.Oommen, P.M.Philip and K.T.Samuel were the teachers in the early period.[40] P.J.Thomas, who had theological training in Serampore College and United Theological College in Bangalore in the beginning of 1940's, [41] encouraged many to have theological education. A number of young men attended the revival meeting held in 1952, dedicated their lives to the service of God and were trained in the Sharon Bible Institute. The students and staff of the Bible school visited a number of places and conducted Bible study classes and it helped to the formation of a few churches in Central Travancore.[42] Though P.J.Thomas has no intention to start a new denomination, a number of pastors began to associate with him, in 1953 at the time of internal strife and division in IPC. The church was further strengthened by the two revival meetings held at Sharon compound in 1953 and 1957. The first revival meeting in December was conducted by a missionary couple called Davood from United States. As a result of miracles, a large crowd of ten thousand people was attracted to the convention

---

[39] C.P.Monai, "Thomachayanum Valarunna Sharonum" (Malayalam) [Thomas and growing Sharon] *Subhavani* [gladtidings], (November, 1992): p.3.

[40] Finny C.Yohannan, "Suvisesha Poralikalude Janma Grihathilekke" (Malayalam) [to the birth place of gospel warriers] *Edayante Sabdam* [Shepherd's voice], 13/2 (June-July, 1996): p.6, 7.

[41] Saju, Kerala Pentecosthu charithram (Malayalam) [History of Pentecostals in Kerala], Kottayam: Goodnews Publications, 1994, p.205.

[42] T.P.Abraham, "Keralathile Penthecosthu Sabhakalude Valarcha" (Malayalam) [growth of Pentecostal churches in Kerala], Achenkunju Elanthoor (ed.), *Unarvinte Jwalakal* [Flames of revival] Kottayam: PPAI, 1992, p.67.

and the meeting was continued for twenty three days on the request of the people. The second great revival meetings were held in March 1957. Rev.John E.Douglas and Rev.Shamback ministered in the meeting and it helped to the progress of the church.[43] The natives who experienced the blessings of the revival went around all the places, preached the Gospel, and established many churches. Many independent churches also joined with Sharon Fellowship Church. Pastor A.A.Cherian, V.G.John, M.D.George, T.M.Varghese were joined with Sharon from the very beginning.

3.2.2. *Progress of the Church*

Those ministers who were dissatisfied to continue in IPC joined with Sharon Fellowship, along with the churches they had influence. The preamble in the memorandum of Sharon Fellowship Church clearly states that it is an association of different churches. "Sharon Fellowship is an association of Pentecostal Churches, Independent Pentecostal Church, Full Gospel Free Church and the churches under the auspicious of Sharon Bible Institute"[44] Therefore it is defined that the Sharon Fellowship Church which organized in 1950's is a fellowship of many independent churches. In 1955 there were about 20 churches which increased to 300 in 1985[45] and 436 in 1992. At present there are about 700 churches[46] in Kerala itself. The most important reason for the success of the Sharon Fellowship Church is the policy of P.J.Thomas to give freedom to the local church to function and administer its own affairs.[47] Aleyamma Thomas who studied in Bangrappatte from 1948 to 51, was the first theological graduate among the Pentecostal

---

[43] V.G.John "Message" *Christian Evangelical Movement Silver Jubliee Souvenier 1957-'82*. Tiruvalla: CEM, 1982, p.3.

[44] *Memmorandum of Sharon Fellowship Church*, 1975, p.1.

[45] Daniel Ayroor, *op.cit.*, p.275.

[46] Information from the office of Sharon Fellowship Church, Tiruvalla in January 1997.

[47] T.A.Abraham, Keralathile Pentecosthu, *op.cit.*, p.68.

women in Kerala and she opened a Bible school for women in 1971. The ladies who studied in this school became a great help to the growth of the church. Church which is progressing under the leadership of P.J. Thomas expanded outside Kerala and North India. Though the church at its beginning enlightened by the revival meeting held by the foreign missionaries, it grew under native leadership. P.J.Thomas had his theological education both in India and abroad had a real vision of indigenous church. Though he received financial support from abroad, as IPC, never subjected to them to be controlled by the foreign mission body. He encouraged many natives to shoulder the church in India and to progress without any foreign domination.

3.2.3. Theological Institutions

Before the formation of Sharon Fellowship Church, Sharon Bible School was started. The students who studied in this school helped much to the formation of many churches in the Sharon Fellowship Church. Faith Theological Seminary, founded in 1970 by Rev.T.G.Koshy, is the first Pentecostal Seminary affiliated to the Senate of Serampore, and it contributed greatly to the theological education of the Pentecostals. At the early period, Pentecostals did not give importance to the theological studies because they thought that theological studies are the intellectual exercise and it will not help to understand scriptural truth. Now the trend has changed and people give importance to theological education. Students from all Pentecostal denominations are given admission in this institution and its impact is felt in all Pentecostal Churches. The seminary is run by the generous contribution of the friends and well-wishers of the institution from India and abroad. A new step has taken place in 1987 to collect an endowment fund so as to meet the financial needs of the seminary by the Indians.[48] According to V.K.Alexander,

---

[48] Samuel Mathew, "Faith Theological Seminary a Short History", *Silver Jubilee Souvenier*, Adur: FTS, 1995, p.35.

the endowment fund secretary, the project is aimed to collect fifty lakh rupees within a period of ten years.[49] Within a period of 3 years more than two lakh rupees was collected from about thousand people who co-operated to the scheme.[50] Seminary also gives importance to the evangelistic activities. For the evangelistic activities of the seminary a fund is collected from the students which is known as 'faith promise'. The target for the academic year 1996-97 was Rs.50,000/-.[51] The fund is used for the evangelistic activities of the students during week-ends and vacations.

All these attempts point towards the growing awareness among the Pentecostals to attain self-sufficiency. Training given in the seminary to meet the needs of their evangelistic activities by themselves help the graduates to implement it in their churches and thus the church shall be improved to find out the sources to meet the needs of evangelistic activities.

3.3. Assemblies of God

Though the Assemblies of God missionaries began to work in South India in 1916, it took an organized form in 1929, with the formation of the South India and Ceylon District Council of the Assemblies of God. The purpose behind its formation was to work in closer co-operation for the general good of the Assemblies of God churches, in this territory and it is hoped that the event will open a new day for the Pentecostal work in South India.[52]

---

[49] V.K.Alexander, "Give And Spend God Will Send". Faith Theological Seminary College Magazine 1989-90, Adur: FTS, 1990, p.28.

[50] V.K.Alexander, "Faith Theological Seminary Endowment Fund", Paricha-College Magazine 1990-91, Adoor: FTS, 1991, p. 49.

[51] Brochure 'Faith-Promise', 1996-97, FTS: Manakala, 1996.

[52] "Report" *Pentecostal Evangel* (July 6, 1929).

3.3.1. *Progress Under Missionary Leadership*

It was the policy of the General Council of the Assemblies of God to develop indigenous churches in every country. According to the decision of the General Council of Assemblies of God held in 1921, it has committed itself to plant self-governing, self-propagating and self-supporting churches abroad.[53] But in South India, it was very slow in implementing the policy of the General Council of Assemblies of God. Till 1947 South India District Council of the Assemblies of God, which was constructed by the missionaries, controlled the churches in South India.[54] Thus during the early period of the Assemblies of God church, it was under the direct control of the missionaries. After the death of Mary.W.Chapman, John.H.Burgess, a young missionary from America took the charge of Assemblies of God churches in Central and South Travancore. The missionaries, Miss.M.C.Ginn (1930), Miss.L.H.Grainer, Mrs.Mary Linberg, Miss.E.Esler, Miss.Martha Kucera were serving the Assemblies of God churches in South India during this period. The natives A.C.Samuel, P.V.John, E.P.Daniel, A.J.John, C.Manasse, R.Samuel, M.C.Chacko also co-operated with the missionaries during this period.

There was a period of stagnation in the Assemblies of God work in Central Travancore due to the separation of R.F.Cook and K.E.Abraham along with the churches and the properties which were under their control.[55] Not discouraged by the separation, they worked along with the new missionaries who arrived in 1930's, concentrated in South Travancore and opened new stations at Trivandrum, Kollarkadavu, Puthupally, Chennithala, Kanartamodi,

---

[53] Assemblies of God, Minutes of the General Council, Missouri, 19-26 August 1921, p.61.

[54] A.C.Samuel, *Assemblies of God* (Malayalam) Trivandrum: Malayalam District of SIAG, 1954, p.26.

[55] *Ibid.*, p.24.

Nellikunnam, Ashtamudi and Cannanore. Most of the adherents of Assemblies of God church during this period were from the other faith background. According to the report found in Pentecostal Evangel ninety percent among the one hundred and fifty member congregation at Trivandrum were from Hinduism.[56] Martha.M.Kucera also reported many conversions from the people of other faiths background.[57] Since early members of A.G.were recently converted to the new faith by the efforts of the missionaries they paid allegiance to the missionaries and were not ready to struggle for an Indian leadership. As caste had an important role in the Indian Society, majority of the members from Hindu background may not want to handover the leadership to a person from Syrian Christian community. Therefore it was very slow to develop an Indian leadership in Assemblies of God Church in Kerala. Though the A.G. work began in Kerala in 1916 none of the Indian brothers were ordained till 1935.[58] It was not the people struggled for native leadership, but the missionaries encouraged the natives to be appointed in the administrative posts.

3.3.1.1. *Bethel Bible College*

At the very early period of their work, missionaries were aware of the difficulties to handle the different climate and the living conditions of the Southern region. Many of the missionaries have become sick and some even left India because of their ill-health. Even in 1912, George Berg expressed the need for two Bible Schools, one in the Nilgiri Mountain and the other in Travancore to train the natives for

---

[56] Carl F.Graves "Encouraging News From South India" *Pentecostal Evangel,* (February, 1933), p.9.

[57] Martha M.Kucera, "Report" *Pentecostal Evangel* (August 19, 1933) cf.*Pentecostal Evangel* (November, 1934), p.13.

[58] L.Sam, *Pastor A.C.Samuel* (Malayalam), Trivandrum: T.J.Rajan, 1983, p.25.

the missionary work.[59] William.M.Faux, the foreign missionary secretary of Assemblies of God who visited South India in 1925, felt the need of a missionary training school in Travancore. Then William.M.Faux who appreciated the work in South India at the 11th General Convention held in United States recommended the council to send more missionaries to South India.[60] Thus the council sent John.H.Burgess as a missionary with an aim to open a Bible School. Thus in 1927, Bethel Bible School was started, with the co-operation of A.J.John, P.V.John and Thalavadi Philip at Mavelikkara,[61] which became a central part in the growth of the Assemblies of God Churches in Kerala. It is the first Bible School which is still in existence, started outside United States. It was according to the decision taken in the General Council of the Assemblies of God held in 1919, to establish Bible schools for the education of duly accredited native workers in the various fields wherever possible.[62] The establishment of the school helped in the growth of Assemblies of God Churches in Travancore. As a result of the ministry of Bible School students, by the end of 1934, fifteen congregations were started in Central Travancore.[63] M. L. Ketcham observes the contribution of Bethel Bible School to the growth of the church thus:

> "Bethel Bible School in Punalur established in 1927 by John H.Burgess, has been largely responsible for the remarkable development of the Assemblies of God in Travancore. Its

---

[59] George E.Berg, "Lights and Shadows in India" *Latter Rain Evangel* (September, 1912), p.14.

[60] 'Report' *Pentecosthu Kahalam* [Pentecostal Trumphet] 1/2 (November, 1925), p.29.

[61] John H. Burgess, "Bethel Bible School" *Bethel Bible School Golden Jubilee Souvenir*, Punalur: Bethel Bible School, 1977, p.3.

[62] Assemblies of God, Minutes of the General Council 1919, p.22, cited in William.W.Menzis, *Anointed to serve the story of the Assemblies of God*, Springfield: The Gospel Publishing House, 1971, p.243.

[63] John H.Burgess "Bible School Proves Blessings" *Pentecostal Evangel* (March 18, 1935), p.6.

graduates have established churches in every corner of Central and South Travancore."[64]

By the establishment of the Bible School many natives could get opportunities to become the leaders. Second World War, which began in 1939, hindered the missionary work in India. During this period there were about six mission stations and twelve missionaries in the Malayalam speaking area. C.T.Maloney says: "The World War II and consequent poverty and financial scarcity badly affected the Assemblies of God church during the period."[65] When war ended in April, 1945 the missionary work became possible again and missionary force increased in the following year. Since nationalism was very prevalent among the Indians, in the following years there were different political changes, which also brought certain changes in the administrative policy of Assemblies of God. The missionaries who were aware of the political changes understood that they have to leave India, if it becomes independent, seriously began to think about the transfer of responsibilities to the natives, and decided to form an administrative council having majority of natives.

3.3.2. *Under Native Leadership [With the Co-operation of Missionaries]*

It was the missionaries, not the natives, who took initiative to transfer the responsibilities to the Indians. After three decades of the ministry of Assemblies of God in South India, the missionaries did find it necessary to handover the responsibilities to the natives. It is very clear from the Report of M.L.Ketcham, "we are encouraging our Indian brothers to get their shoulders under the wheel and to establish

---

[64] M.L.Ketcham, "Travancore" *The Missionary Challenge* (January, 1954):p.18.

[65] C.T.Maloney, Report on South India and Ceylon presented in the missionary conference held at Springfield, (March 16-18, 1943), 7 (Unpublished)

themselves as self-supporting, self-propagating, institutions in Christ Jesus."[66]

In order to organize the work in South India, it is decided to form District Councils for each of the four language areas viz. Malayalam, Tamil, Marathi and Telugu and a general conference to unite all the work into one body.[67] Therefore in the year 1947 steps were taken to form a national organization and it was registered in 1949 at Bombay by the name 'South India Assemblies of God'(SIAG) and was administered by a council which has natives in majority.[68] Carl D.Holleman was chosen as the first superintendent and he served, till 1954. Holleman too insisted that the natives should take the responsibility. He states: "When the organization has been completed and the SIAG was registered with the government, I insisted that a national should take the leadership, in all areas of SIAG. A.C.Samuel was elected General Superintendent and served from 1954."[69] According to the constitution of SIAG, Article III Section 3: "Indian brothers shall be in majority on the General executive committee. At least one of the offices, of the Superintendent or Assistant Superintendent, shall be held by an Indian brother."[70]

Though the administrative responsibility of the church is handed over to the natives in the wake of Indian independence, the presence of missionaries and their influence in the administration of the church were felt in the state till 1979. When the Malayalam District council was formed in 1947,

---

[66] M.L.Ketcham "Church in Progress" *Pentecostal Evangel* (February 5, 1938): p.7.

[67] Benjamin Prasad Shinde, *"The contribution of the Assemblies of God to church Growth in India"* M.A.Thesis, Fuller Theological Seminary, 1974 (unpublished), pp.123, 124.

[68] A.C.Samuel, *op.cit,* p.26.

[69] Carl.D.Holleman, *South India,* 1978 (unpublished), p.16.

[70] The constitution and by-laws of the SIAG, Punalur: Planters printing and Publishing House, 1956, pp.6, 7.

John H.Burgess was elected as its first superintendent and served till 1949. Then A.C.Samuel became the first Indian who served as superintendent till 1967 and he was succeeded by C.Kunjummen who continued in the post till his death in 1979.

When the native leadership emerged, it was unable to give a regular financial support to the ministers due to the lack of fund and increase of ministers. But it helped to develop a strong sense of responsibility among the members of the church to support their pastors. Thus the indigenous church principle was operating with some degree of success in the Assemblies of God churches in Kerala during this period.[71]

The main source of income of the church is the tithe[72] given by the members of the church to support the pastor. According to the sections I, article VIII of the constitution of SIAG "church members should be taught and strongly encouraged to pay their tithes into the local church for the support of the pastor. The pastors are obliged to pay their tithes to the District Treasury and each District should contribute part of its income to the office of SIAG to meet the needs of General office."[73] Thus church the has developed into a stage to maintain its own affairs without depending on the missionaries was an important step in the growth of AG Church.

Another important step taken during the period was the transfer of properties to the natives. All the properties bought earlier were registered to the council of Assemblies of God. In many of the mission societies transfer of property has become a great problem between natives and missionaries. Since the formation of SIAG, the church properties were bought in the name of the respective District of the South

---

[71] Mathew P.Scariah "An Evaluation of The History of The Assemblies of God Churches in Kerala And Proposals For The Unity Among The Pentecostal Churches in Kerala" M.Th.Thesis, Senate of Serampore College, 1996 (unpublished), pp.98,99.

[72] Tithe-means one tenth of the total income.

[73] Constitution and By-laws of A.G., 1954, p.15.

India Assemblies of God. In March 1973, all the properties hitherto held by the General Council of the Assemblies of God USA were also deeded to the Indian Church.[74]

Thus by 1990's Assemblies of God church in Kerala, developed under native leadership, to be fully controlled and supported by the natives. It largely helped to the progress of the church in the following years.

Home Missionary Council (HMC), founded by the students and faculty of Bethel Bible School, has played an important role for the establishment of many churches during this period. It is purely an indigenous organ, collecting funds from local churches and well-wishers, to work in unreached areas. Foreign missionaries do not have any direct or indirect involvement in any of the activities of it. Seventy five percent of Assemblies of God Churches in Malabar were formed by the missionary activities of the Home Missionary Council.[75]

T.C.George who analyzed the church growth from 1975 to 79 says that AG had tremendous growth both in the number of believers and churches in South India during this period. It noticed an increase of 43 percent in membership and 33 percent in number of churches.[76]

According to T.C.George the reason for the remarkable growth is the application and implementation of church growth principles such as make churches indigenous, multiply house churches, and advocate minimum social dislocation. Concerning the indigenous aspects, he says, without waiting for a long time to get permission from headquarters of the denomination Pentecostals can begin new congregation.[77] About it Heinrich Schafer says: "The traditional church is

---

[74] Benjamin Prasad Shinde, *op.cit.*, p.183.

[75] M.S.Mathai, "Home Missionary Council" *Bethel Bible School Golden Jubliee Souvenir*, Punalur: Bethel Bible School, 1977, pp.16, 17.

[76] T.C.George, "Pentecostal Church Growth in South India", *Church Growth Quarterly* 3/3 (January-March, 1981): p.138.

[77] *Ibid.*, pp.138-139.

declining because a priest cannot do anything without the decision of the committee while 'Pentecostals do not need a committee to regulate everything first."[78]

By the active evangelistic activities during this period, under the leadership of A.C.Samuel and C.Kunjummen and with the close co-operation of missionaries from United States, number of churches in South India Assemblies of God increased to 366 in 1979 from 115 in 1952. The number of churches in Malayalam District also increased from 65(1952) to 192(1979). According to a report in 1977 every month the Malayalam District was successful in pioneering about two new churches.[79]

3.3.3. *Under Native Leadership [Without the Interference of Missionaries]*

By 1979, when the last missionary Earl Stubbs too left, the Malayalam field was left without any missionaries. During this period the Assemblies of God Church progressed under the native leadership without having any missionary interference.

P.D.Johnson succeeded C.Kunjummen in 1979, as superintendent, and played a remarkable role in the development of the church. While he was the superintendent, in 1982 the Assemblies of God work in Kerala was renamed as Malayalam District of the Assemblies of God, at the formation of the Southern District of Assemblies of God.[80] While P.D.Johnson was the superintendent the General

---

[78] Heinrich Schafer, *Church Identity Between Repression and Liberation: The Presbyterian Church in Guatimala,* trans. by Craij Koslofsky (Geneva: WARC, 1991), p.45.

[79] C.Earl Stubbs. "Golden Jubilee" *Pentecostal witness* (March, 1977): p.11.

[80] T.J.Samuel, The *Origin and Development of Assemblies of God in Kerala,* presented in All-Indian General Conference of AG in Delhi (February, 1995), p.2.

Convention was started, the constitution and by-laws were revised and prepared for the administration of the local church.[81] During his period the number of churches increased from 192(in 1979) to 304(in 1990). Here we find an increase of 112 churches within a period of eleven years. It points that about ten churches were added every year.

T.J.Samuel succeeded P.D.Johnson after his death in 1990, gave active leadership to the church till 1996. In the beginning of 1990's we find a tremendous growth. Many churches were established at Central and Northern part of Kerala. During this period, in order to conduct general convention, a ground was purchased in Punalur town with the money collected from the natives. When it was announced on Sunday, third February 1991, two lakh rupees were collected on the spot was a great encouragement.[82] It has proven that now the churches in Kerala are self-sufficient and they are able to meet the needs by themselves.

A mission board was formed in 1994, to give the local church more vision about mission. As a result of various meeting held to enlarge the missionary vision about 1000 people pledged to give regular financial support. According to the policy of Mission Board, each member of the church is asked to give one rupee each month to the missionary work.[83] Seven missionaries were also sent to North India by the Malayalam District Assemblies of God in 1994. These all point

---

[81] L.Sam, "Assemblies of God Nethakkanmar" (Malayalam) [Leaders of Assemblies of God] K.J.Mathew and Finny George (eds.), Kristhiya Sabha charithram Oru Padanam Noottandukaliloode (Malayalam) [A study of the history of Christianity through centuries], Punalur: SIAG Malayalam District Council 1996, p.123.

[82] Shibu Thomas, "Assemblies of God General Convention" (Malayalam), *Swargeeya Dwani* [Heavenly Echo], (February, 1991): p.4.

[83] P.S.Philip, "Puthuvarshathilekke Pratheekshakalode" [to the new year, with expectations] *Swargeeya Dwani* [Heavenly Echo], (January, 1994), p.9.

towards the new awareness of mission developed under native leadership.

3.3.4. *The General Council of the Assemblies of God in India*

During very early period 1970's attempts were made to the formation of the general council of the Assemblies of God to provide an extensive fellowship and co-operation between the three separate councils of different regions in India, viz. South India Assemblies of God, Assemblies of God of North India, and Assemblies of God of North East India. An Adhoc Committee was constituted with the representatives from the leaders of the three regions to give directions to the formation of it.[84] But the general council of the Assemblies of God of India was officially constituted in February 1995 at New Delhi meeting, and Rev.Y.Jeyaraj and T.J.Samuel were elected as All India General Superintendent and Secretary respectively. At present there are 3300 churches in India.[85]

In 1980's and 1990's we find an amazing progress in the number of churches all over India, especially in the Malayalam District of the Assemblies of God. It is mainly because of implementing indigenous principle in the church. Mathew P.Skariah comments about this period thus:

> "During this period (1979-1996) the church neither received any financial support from the Foreign Mission Department of the Assemblies of God in United States of America, nor had any missionary supervision here. But the work expanded to a great extend through the enormous contributions and sacrificial giving of the nationals. The teaching of the 'tithe giving' was prevalent in the church."[86]

---

[84] Yesudian Jeyaraj, "From the chairman" The General Council of the Assemblies of God of India Bullettin (February, 1995), p.4.

[85] "Assemblies of God Convention Eee Azhchayil (Malayalam) [Assemblies of God Convention in this week] Halelujah 2/2 (February 15, 1996): p.1.

[86] Mathew P.Skariah, *op.cit.*, p.104.

At the early period of native leadership, since it was a period of transferring responsibilities, Assemblies of God was slow in its progress. Therefore Indian Pentecostal Church of God, which was founded and developed under the native leadership, progressed to be the highest in number as compared with other churches. As earlier cited there are different reasons, firstly AG had a set back from central Travancore in 1929, where Syrian Christians are having influence. Therefore IPC, dominated by Syrian Christians, have thorough knowledge in the scripture could spread the teaching to the neighbouring villages. Many of those who had Syrian Christian background set out to do the missionary work at very early 1930's, while AG work was controlled by foreign missionaries, who do not have easy access to the natives.

Secondly, when the leadership responsibilities were transferred from missionaries to the natives it progressed slowly because it took much time to adjust with the new situation. In the book *Verdict Theology in Missionary Anthropology*, Dr.Alan R.Tippet rightly said: "It is much easier to start a church on indigenous principles than it is to change over from a long established paternalistic enclosed mission station congregation."[87]

It is very clear from the history of the development of indigenous leadership in Assemblies of God Church that though the churches had found it difficult to grow in the early stages, due to its pervious dependence upon the missionary society for everything, progressed when the indigenous principles implemented to the church. In India, especially in Kerala, only the church under indigenous leadership will progress because Malayalees have a desire to be independent and retain an anti-missionary feeling.

---

[87] Alan R.Tippett, *Verdict Theology in Missionary Anthoropology*, South Pasadena: William Carey Library, 1973, p.151.

3.4. Church of God [Full Gospel] in India

Robert F.Cook, an independent Pentecostal missionary from America came to Travancore in 1914, established few congregations known as 'Full Gospel Church in Malabar' [*Malankara Poorna Suvisesha Sabha*] became an affiliated missionary of Assemblies of God in 1919 and continued in that relation till 1929. Then he worked as an independent missionary till he joined with Church of God, Cleveland, Tennesse in 1936. Following Cook, many other missionaries like William Posphil, Paul Cook, Dora P.Myers, French etc., worked along with the natives, T.M.Varghese, A.K.Varghese, Gnanaprakasham, ART Athisayam, E.V.George, etc. At different occasions there were struggle for the leadership. The first struggle was in 1948 between Cook and other missionaries. Then the second one was for the equal representation of depressed class which resulted in a division. The third leadership struggle occurred in 1993 which was healed ony at end of the century. Though the natives are appointed to official positions, still the church is controlled from its head quarters, Cleveland, Tennesse is a major drawback of the church.

3.4.1. Period from 1930-1936

R.F.Cook along with K.E.Abraham severed his relation with Assemblies of God in 1929 due to some of the reasons stated earlier, and began to work independently. At the beginning of 1930, K.E.Abraham and his co-workers too left Cook by the influence of Paul of Ceylon. Most of the members in the 40 churches stood along with Cook[88] were from the depressed class. Cook and his churches have gone through financial crisis during this period. About it Cook says that thirty co-workers faithfully supported Cook and his churches in South India, dropped out one by one owing to the depression in the United

---

[88] Sunny P.Samuel (ed.), "Daivasabha Charithram" (Malayalam) [History of Church of God] Churches of God in India Kerala State General Convention Souvenir, Mulakkuzha: State Council of CGI, 1996, p.12.

States, leaving only five supporters in 1932. The support that comes around thirty dollars was divided among twenty six workers, some receiving only fifty cents, some a dollar, while the more able workers usually received two to three dollars a month.[89]

During the period of financial crisis Cook exhorted the ministers to stand in faith; and it helped them to turn their eyes from the missionary to God whom they are serving.[90] Though the people were poor, they supported the preachers and their family with what they had. Bartha N.Cook writes in her Diary: "The saints, though poor, gave an offering of coconuts and pineapples and sent fifty four eggs."[91] She again writes: "At the close of the meetings tender coconuts... were presented and eight eggs were given to me; Though they are very poor, they like to give us eggs and sometimes we get a good number when we visit them."[92]

While Cook and his co-workers were suffering and struggling for the existence, Indian Pentecostal Church of God leaders, K.E.Abraham and K.C.Cherian could establish relationship with Swedish Church, through Carl Swan, obtained an opportunity to visit Sweden. Cook who understood it thought that it will become a threat to, his work tried to prevent their visit to foreign countries. Cook was not successful in his attempt to prevent their journey and much worried about the future of his work in the new situation. About it Cook himself writes:

> "Since two of the brethren of the Indian Pentecostal Church of God were taken to a Foreign country, we sensed the danger that lay ahead on their return, especially if they were backed

---

[89] Robert F.Cook, *Half a Century of Divine Leading And 37 years of Apostolic Achievements In South India,* Tennesse: Church of God, 1955, pp.206, 207.

[90] *Ibid.*

[91] Bartha N.Cook, "Diary" (September 22, 1929) cited in Mammen Philip, *op.cit.,* p.137.

[92] Robert F.Cook, *op. cit.,* p.247.

> by foreign finances; so we trusted the Lord for divine guidance
> and help for the future of the work."[93]

While Cook was worrying about the situation, some of the brethren advised him to affiliate the churches to a foreign body that holds the full Gospel truth. Cook who did not know any Pentecostal organization, other than Assemblies of God, interested in the missionary work of 'third world countries', could meet brother J.H.Ingram, a representative of the Church of God with head quarters at Cleveland, Tennesse, at Nilgiri Hills through an Indian lace merchant in 1936. After going through the teachings and minutes of the Church of God, and after much thought and prayer, arranged a general body meeting of 'Full Gospel Church in Malabar' on 15th May 1936. Ministers and representatives from 51 churches (except two) under Cook attended the meeting, unanimously decided to join with Church of God, Cleveland, Tennessee by changing its name as 'Church of God [Full Gospel] in India.'[94] In 1936, together with Mount Zion Bible School and sixty three Churches with its 2537 members joined with Church of God, Cleveland.[95]

Thus Cook and his churches progressing independently joined with a foreign body by the compulsion of the situation- to fight against Swedish money power. The church which was striving forward to indigenous principles by dropping the supporters one by one was again under the foreign domination. While K.E.Abraham and his co-workers could obtain financial assistance without any foreign domination, Cook and his churches came under the control of foreign mission body. The whole situation was created by the financial

---

[93] *Ibid.*, p.211.

[94] T.M.Varghese and E.V.George, *Daivasabha Pinnitta Anpathu Varshangal* (Malayalam) [The last fifty years of the church of God] Mulakkuzha: CGI Literature Service, 1973, p.29.

[95] Charles W.Conn, *Like a Mighty Army.* Tennesse: Church of God Publishing House, 1955, p.236.

assistance sought by the natives from abroad. So when we analyze the situation, foreign connection gave always more troubles to the Indian churches.

3.4.2.   *Period Under Missionary Leadership [1936-1970]*

Churches which joined along with Cook to Church of God in 1936 came under the direct control of Church of God, Cleveland. The World Mission Department of the Church of God continues to retain considerable control over the daughter churches abroad.[96] It is very clearly stated in the policy of the Church of God in India, published in 1976. According to it:

> "...the church of God (Full Gospel) in India is, and shall be governed by the current acts, teachings, discipline and the government of the General Assembly of the Church of God International with offices Located at Keith at 25th N.W.Cleveland, Tennesse, 37311, USA."[97]

The field representative or the state overseer is appointed and paid by the Foreign Mission Board and the duties and responsibilities entrusted upon him are subjected to the control of the same. "The state overseer shall make monthly reports to the general overseer on forms prepared for such reports and before launching large financial state projects, he is to have the approval of the General Executive Committee."[98] The one who is able to influence the General Overseer is appointed to the post. It has many practical difficulties and the recent struggle in leadership is an outcome of such a policy.

---

[96] Gary. B.McGee, "The Azusa Street Revival and Twentieth-Century Missions" *International Bulletin of Missionary Research* (April, 1988): p.61.

[97] Supplement to the General Assembly minutes and Church of God (Full Gospel) India Policy, India: CGI Press, p.71.

[98] *Ibid.,* p.42, 43.

3.4.2.1. Cook – *The First Missionary [1936-1950]*

When Cook and his churches joined with Church of God Cleveland, Cook was appointed as the first missionary of the organization. Cook was able to give a regular support to the ministers and built many churches and cemeteries, with the financial support obtained from the headquarters.

Cook who longed to work and live in India till his death, was not permitted by the Mission Department. So, there was a crisis occurred between C.E.French and Cook and there were two groups, one favouring Cook and another favouring French. About it T.M.Varghese writes: it became an opportunity to satan. Co-workers of Cook began to fight each other forming separate groups and tried to remove Cook from his position. Many unhappy events occurred in the church.[99] For the progress of the church, T.M.Varghese, the Field Secretary, favoured C.E.French and it helped the church to continue in relation with Church of God.[100] It was according to the policy of the Church of God World Mission that a person can only be in a place for twelve years. Therefore C.E.French was sent to Travancore in 1947 to take the charge of the work, when Cook completed his twelve years period in 1948. General Overseer Rev. Chesser and Secretary Rev. Walker were sent by the Mission Board, to solve the problem and R.F.Cook was called back to United States in 1950.

There were people who hold the opinion that, they should not depend on foreign sources to the progress of the work which will bring troubles like this. In a conference of ministers that belonged to both groups Pastor C.G.Varghese said: "We face troubles because of seeking springs and river side for

---

[99] T.M.Varghese and E.V.George, *op.cit.,* p.30.

[100] John Mathew, "Pastor T.M.Varghese *Suvesesha Dwani* [Gospel Echo], 12/101, (October, 1972): p.21 .

the benefit of a few people. Therefore turn our eyes from the West and trust in God."[101]

T.M.Varghese, favoured the decisions of Mission Board and gave support to C.E.French, insisted the church to continue in relation to Church of God in Cleveland. Thus the churches continued, without breaking away from Foreign Mission Board.

3.4.2.2. Church in the Process of Development [1950-1970]

Though the church was joined with Church of God in Cleveland in 1936, it continued without any change under the control of Cook till 1948. But by the coming of more missionaries, the situation changed. C.E.French, as the Missionary overseer after R.F.Cook in 1948, could bring the churches in India under the centralized government.[102] In 1949 church was registered at Coimbatore under the Society Act of 1860, and properties at sixty six places bought in the name of Cook was deeded to Church of God [Full Gospel] in India.[103] Thus C.E.French laid a firm foundation for the church to progress in relation to Church of God, Cleveland and returned to United States due to his ill health in 1952.

Following C.E.French, William Pospisil and family came to India in 1952 served as a missionary for twenty years till 1972. During his period he brought about many administrative changes and built many churches. It was his plan to divide the church in India into states, to give regional representation, and that helped the growth of the church. The missionaries, Miss. Dora. P. Myers (1950-1965), Mrs. & Mr. Robert J. Reecer (1964-1970), Rev. Darel. L. Lindsey (1967-1969), Rev. H. L.

---

[101] John Mathew, Pastor C.G.Varghese (Malayalam) Suvesesha Dwani 12/111 (November, 1972): p.15.

[102] Sunny P.Samuel, *op.cit.,* p.19.

[103] T.M.Varghese, *op.cit.,* p.31.

Termer (1957-1963) also served in India in their various capacities,[104] co-operating with the natives; such as A.K. Varghese, T.M. Varghese Gnanaprakasam, A.R.T. Athisayam and Benjamin.[105]

Since Cook identified himself with the poor people in the society, many from the depressed class joined with him. They did not have any hope of social uplift in any Christian denomination due to the caste discrimination, many joined with Pentecostal groups which proclaim baptism in Holy Spirit irrespective of caste.[106] But the missionaries after Cook did not show much concern to them. So, they felt that they are not treated as equals with Syrian Christians. So, they argued for equal status with the Syrian Christians in administration, and at last it resulted in a division. Thus in 1972 Church of God in Kerala was divided into two, Church of God in Kerala [Division], and the Church of God in Kerala [State] to give administrative responsibilities to the people from the depressed classes.[107]

During the days of missionaries, i.e., from 1936 to 1970, they served as missionary overseers and natives served as the field representatives. From 1936 to 1966 T.M.Varghese served as field representative. When T.M.Varghese retired in 1966, P.A.V.Sam was appointed as the field representative, till 1970.[108] When autonomy was given in 1970 the post of field representative was dissolved.

---

[104] *Ibid.*, pp.56-66.

[105] Dora P.Myers, *Daiva Sabha Charithram* (Malayalam) [History of the Church of God], Mulakkuzha: CGI Press, p.59.

[106] K.J.Mathew, Denominational Pluralism Among the Pentecostals in Kerala, Causes and Responses, 1920 to The Present", M.Th.Thesis, Senate of Serampore College, 1993 (unpublished), pp.90, 91.

[107] T.M.Varghese, *op. cit.*, pp.43, 44.

[108] Sunny P.Samuel (ed.), *op.cit.*, p.23.

3.4.3. *Church Under State Representatives [From 1970 onwards]*

Till 1962, all churches in India were administered from the headquarters at Mulakkuzha, Chengannur. In 1962, the church was divided into three states, viz. Kerala, Madras and Andhra on the regional basis to give regional representation. In 1966, one more state was added known as North India Fields. Each state was administered by a missionary overseer and a state representative. Pastor U.Thomas (1964-1966) and Pastor P.C.Chacko (1966-1970) served as state representatives under William Pospisil (1952-1972) the missionary overseer. But in 1970 autonomy was given to the states for the administration of the church. Though there were state representatives from 1962 to 1970 they did not have any power to exercise. Pastor A.V.Abraham (1970-1978) and Pastor M.V.Chacko (1978-1988) served in the office as state overseers.[109]

According to the statistics available the number of churches has increased from 63 in 1936 to 359 in 1993.[110] Therefore 296 churches were added within a period of 57 years that is 5.2 churches were added every year. Comparing to the growth of other denominations it is much slow in progress.

Major drawback of this organization is that, though the state representative (overseer) is selected from the natives, they are appointed, and paid from the General Office in Cleveland, Tennessee. For most of the needs they have to depend upon foreign sources. States overseer is not allowed to start any project without the permission from General Executive Committee. Since general overseer, who takes

---

[109] *Ibid.,* pp.22-24.
[110] T.P.Abraham, *Keralathile Pentecosthu......op.cit.,* p.63.

important decisions concerning the church in Kerala, are not aware of the culture, practices and notions of the people in Kerala, and were often influenced by the one who is able to please him. The general overseer, who stays abroad, delays decisions due to practical difficulties. Most often the decision may not be appropriate to the situation also (1972 events, 1993...). So, it is necessary to give power and authority to an Indian to take decisions and to control the church. If it comes fully under Indian leadership, church will be able to take the appropriate decision in time which helps to the progress of the church.

CHAPTER IV

Impact of Indigenous Leadership

Indigenous leadership that emerged among the Indian Pentecostal Church of God by 1930 had a lasting impact in the development of the Pentecostal churches in Kerala. The remarkable growth of the church during the period strengthened many others to strive towards the native leadership. Under the Indian leadership natives became more responsible in the church affairs than they acted in the period in which missionaries controlled the work. Missionaries were handicapped by imperfect command of the language while native leaders who are thorough in language, culture and aspirations of the people were able to take the decision suitable to the situation. The immense growth under indigenous leadership challenged many others to follow the same and hence many independent churches were formed which became helpful for the increase of the Pentecostal churches in Kerala.[1] Some of the important contributions of the indigenous leadership can be noted as follows: (1) Indigenous leadership helped to the remarkable growth of the Pentecostal churches in Kerala. (2) It helped to develop indigenous principles such as self-support, self-propagation, etc. (3) It became a unifying

---

[1] Babu George, "Einiyum Presthanangal Untakatte" (Malayalam) [let there be more organizations], *Swargeeya Dwani* [Heavenly Echo], (July, 1992): p.3.

T.P.Abraham, "Puthiya Presthangal Einiyum Avasyamo?" (Malayalam) [is there any need for new organizations], *Swargeeya Dwani* [Heavenly Echo], (May, 1996): p.2.

factor to the church which were progressing independently. (4) Indian leadership could help to develop an Indian identity among Pentecostal churches. (5) It helped to the progress in the field of theological education and (6) It helped to the progress of missionary work.

4.1. Growth of the Church

South Indian Pentecostal Church of God, established in 1923 under native leadership and registered in 1935 by the name Indian Pentecostal Church of God, had only about fifty churches in 1936. Church under the native leadership of P.M.Samuel, K.E.Abraham, T.G.Oommen and P.L.Paramjyothi progressed to 3300 churches by 1997.[2] The progress is continuing under the leadership of K.M.Joseph who succeeded Paramjyothi in 1996. Churches in Malayalam speaking region is administered by Indian Pentecostal Church of God Kerala State Council, is having about 1750 churches. It also progress under the native leadership of M.V.Chacko, K.M.John, and K.C.John who are president, vice-president and secretary respectively. In the past as well as the present, Indian Pentecostal Church of God is the leading Pentecostal denomination in Kerala.[3]

It is a generally accepted fact that the efficient leadership of K.E.Abraham, was the secret behind the growth of Indian Pentecostal Church of God. About it his biographer Habel.G.Varghese says: Pastor Abraham's contribution to the Pentecostal movement in India in general and to the Indian Pentecostal Church of God in particular are great and far reaching.[4]

---

[2] T.S.Abraham, "Kumbanad Convention Innarambikkunnu" (Malayalam) [Kumbanad convention begins today], Malayala Manorama (Daily), Kottayam: (January 12, 1997), p.5.

[3] P.D.Johnson, *Vagdatha Nivarthy* (Malayalam) [the promise fulfilled], Trivandrum: P.D.Johnson, 1968,129, cf.K.J.Mathew, *op.cit.*, P.Scariah, *op.cit*, p.118.

[4] Habel G.Varghese, *K.E.Abraham: An Apostle From Modern India*, Kandampanad: The Christian Literature Service in India, 1974, p.105.

Therefore it is clear that it was the native leadership of the people like K.E.Abraham, helped to the growth of Pentecostal Churches in Kerala. By the seventy three years of its mission Indian Pentecostal Church of God could establish 1750 churches in Kerala, shows an average growth of twenty four churches every year, and it is a remarkable progress which no other denomination can claim.

We can see a tremendous growth in the number of churches in other denomination also which functions under native leadership. Sharon Fellowship Church organized by P.J.Thomas in 1953 could establish about 700 churches by 44 years of its mission in Kerala.[5] It shows that about sixteen churches were established every year. Assemblies of God churches established by the efforts of foreign missionaries have also progressed under the native leadership since 1949. When the responsibilities were transferred, though it was slow in its progress at first, we find tremendous growth in the recent years. The numbers of churches were increased from 65 in 1952 to 192 in 1979.[6] With twenty seven years of its ministry we find only an increase of 127 churches that is 4.7 churches every year. But when even the last missionary left the field in 1979, we find a remarkable growth under the leadership of P. D. Johnson, T.J.Samuel and P.S.Philip and the number of churches reached upto 550 in 1997.[7] By the 18 years of its history we find an increase of 358 churches i.e., twenty churches every year. Therefore it is clear that the church progressed more under native leadership than under missionary leadership. But T.J.Samuel has the opinion that the early period, under the missionary leadership, was a formative period and the missionaries laid a firm foundation

---

[5] Information obtained from the head office of Sharon Fellowship Church, Tiruvalla, on 28th January, 1997.

[6] A.C.Samuel, *op.cit.*, p.27, cf and Daniel Airoor, *op.cit.*, p.49.

[7] Assemblies of God Convention (Malayalam), *Hallelujah* (January, 1997), p.1.

with the co-operation of the natives on which the natives could build and so the contributions of the missionaries are very important.[8]

Full Gospel church in Malabar led by Cook had 63 churches when it joined with Church of God, Cleveland. This is more in number than other organization - IPC and AG. But it is not progressed as much as the other denominations. In 1985 there were only 190 churches[9] and it increased to 220 in 1988.[10] Only 220 churches were established by the seventy four years of its ministry i.e., only three churches every year. One of the main reasons for the slowness of its progress is its dependence on foreign mission body. The state representatives had been elected from the natives since 1962 and governed by the missionary overseer. But, from 1970 onwards, they appointed natives to the post of state overseers to implement the decentralization policy of Church of God,[11] still the appointment and payment made by the headquarters of the church in Cleveland is a hindrance to the development of the church. Foreign missionary control over the church often caused difficulties to take appropriate decision in time and many of the decisions may not be appropriate to the situations. Thus the church did not show as much progress as the other denominations had in the previous years.

From the statistics available concerning the growth of the Pentecostal churches in Kerala, it is clear that the church under native leadership (IPC and Sharon) had a remarkable growth while the churches which transferred its leadership

---

[8] Interview with T.J.Samuel at his residence in Punalur on 12th November, 1996.

[9] "India Daivasabha Kerala State Convention", *Goodnews* (February 6, 1985), p.3.

[10] Sunny P.Samuel (ed.), "Daivasabha Charithram" (Malayalam) [History of the Church of God], *India Poorna Suvisesha Daivasabha General Convention Souvenir* [Church of God (Full Gospel) in India General Convention souvenir], Mulakkuzha: State Council, 1996, p.26.

[11] *Ibid.*, p.24

responsibilities from the missionaries to the natives (AG) was slow in its progress at first, but showed much progress after a few years. The church which had come under the mission body (Church of God) was slow in its progress. Therefore it is very plain that the native leadership contributed to the growth of the Pentecostal churches in Kerala, and the independent step taken by the natives in early 1930's could challenge others too.

4.2.   Self-Sufficiency

Under the native leadership there were serious attempts to maintain their affairs by themselves, while churches under the missionary leadership always depend upon their mission body to meet their needs. Church under native leadership always emphasized that it is the responsibility of the church to meet their needs by themselves and it is clear from the teachings of K.E.Abraham. He asked the congregations to meet the needs of their pastors and requested the ministers not to depend on the money that is provided by a missionary agent but trust in God for every needs.[12]

The main source of income for the support of the pastor is the tithe offered by the members of the church. If there are not less than ten families, a pastor is able to be supported by the congregation to live in the average status of the people. If there are more than ten families, rest of the amount can be used for buying property and maintenance of the church building and to conduct evangelistic campaign etc. Since the expense of the pastor is less than that of a foreign missionary it is not very difficult for a congregation to meet it. Cook writes about a congregation of Aaramada [4 kms from Trivandurm] led by Kochukunju Vidyar, which maintain its own affairs from the generous contribution of the members of the church and they conducted four conventions spending

---

12 K.E.Abraham, "Suvisesha Parisramam…", *Zion Kahalam* [Zion Trumphet], 2/2 & 3, 3(February-March, 1938); p.68.

about five hundred rupees a year, in 1929. They do not receive any financial support from any foreign mission, but they are trained to give for the church after spending very little for their livelihood.[13]

Though Indian Pentecostal Church of God entered into Swedish relation in 1936 and missionary tour of Indian leaders to Sweden and America helped to obtain financial support to own properties at different places, they emphasized the natives to maintain its affairs by themselves. There are people who do not find any fault in receiving help from foreign mission body.[14] According to E.V.George, "there is no harm in receiving foreign money if they are not requesting any report. If they ask any report it is better not to receive the money because it may become a cause for exploitation.[15] The main emphasis is to move forward to self-support. Financial status of the Pentecostals in Kerala is improved and now they are able to raise the needed fund. Samuel Mathew observes: "The church is improving in its financial resources and attempts have also been made to attain self-support for the ministry here."[16]

One of such attempts found success in the Assemblies of God Church during this period was the purchase of convention ground at Punalur. When the need for a convention ground was announced in the last day of convention in February 1991 by T.J.Samuel, the superintendent of Malayalam District, about two lakh rupees were collected from the natives

---

[13] Robert F.Cook, "Thekken Thiruvathamkur convention (Malayalam) [Convention in South Travancore], *Suvisesha Prabhashakan* [full Gospel Preacher], 2/8 & 9(March-April, 1929): pp.227, 228.

[14] Achankunja Elanthoor, *Penthecosthukarodu Mathram* (Malayalam) [only to the Pentecostals], Tiruvalla: Deepthi Books, 1991, p.19.

[15] Interview with Pastor E.V.George at his residence Edemon, (Punalur), on 12th November, 1996.

[16] Samuel Mathew, The Pentecostal Churches in Kerala and its witness in the Socio-political Life, M.Th.Thesis, Kottayam: F.F.R.R.C., 1990 (Unpublished), p.85.

on the spot itself.[17] It is because of the awareness of the responsibility of the people helped to contribute towards the needs of the church. Thus Pentecostal churches in Kerala are developing to achieve self-support. Most of the training institutions are run by the financial assistance from abroad. But in recent years, there are attempts to finance the training institutions by raising fund from natives. For example, Herbron Bible College is run by IPC State Council, an endowment fund scheme introduced by Faith Theological Seminary[18] etc. There are also remarkable collections from the Pentecostal churches for charitable works. Thus we find an amazing progress in the area of self support in running institutions, doing charitable works and maintaining church affairs.

Pentecostals gave much importance to the propagation of the gospel, even from the very beginning of the movement. It was for this purpose the Bible Schools were started. All the Bible Schools-Bethel, Mount Zion, Herbron, Sharon etc.-train natives for the propagation of the gospel. In Hebron Bible College and Mount Zion Bible Institute, classes were held during the period of monsoon from June to September in which no evangelistic activities are possible.[19] Students of the Bible School were much used for the propagation of the gospel. Students and staff of Bethel Bible College in Punalur established Home Missionary Council in 1952 to propagate the gospel in unreached area. The fund for it was collected from the friends and students. An inter-denominational organization named Salem Tract Society was established for the printing and distribution of tracts in 1960. The intention behind its formation was to use the Indian means to evangelize

---

[17] Shibu Thomas, "Assemblies of God Convention" (Malayalam), *Swargeeya Dwani*, (February, 1991), p.4.

[18] See above page nos.73 & 78.

[19] "Bible School" (Malayalam), *Suvisesha Prabhashakan* [The Full Gospel Preacher], 2/10 & 11(May-June, 1929): 267, and T.G.Oommen, *op.cit.*, p.35.

India. According to V.M.Mathew, "We should share the gospel truth to the Indians, who oppose the foreign domination, as the men of this soil."[20] Thus under native leadership there was a growing awareness among the members of the Pentecostal churches to propagate the gospel among the natives by using the Indian means.

4.3. Unifying Factor

There were many who desired to progress independently without having foreign missionary dominion. When the natives separated from missionary control and formed church under native leadership, many independent congregations who dislike missionary control joined with the church under native leadership. Thus the indigenous leadership became a unifying factor for many independent Pentecostal churches. For example, P.M.Samuel and Kochukunju Vaidyar joined with K.E.Abraham along with their churches. The independence of the local church as in the New Testament pattern offered by the Indian leadership attracted many who stood for the independence from foreign body to join with native leadership. According to the administrative policy of IPC, power and authority is given to the local church and an apostle will be there to help in the ministry, who is only a fellow-servant or co-worker. This policy of the early leaders pleased the people, who had legitimate desire for freedom and they joined with them which strengthened the Pentecostal churches in Travancore. Hence the indigenous leadership that emerged in the beginning of 1930 became largely a unifying force for the Pentecostal Churches in Kerala.

In later period also the Indian Pentecostal leaders attempted to unite the churches. Usually the Western policy is to divide and rule, while the natives desire for unity. When the Assemblies of God decided to hand over the

---

[20] V.M.Mathew, "Ee Verum Chilave Enthine?" (Malayalam) [Why should the money be wasted?], *Salem Tract Society Silver Jubilee Souvenir*, Vakathanam: Salem Tract Society, 1985, p.98.

responsibilities to the natives in 1947, Indian leaders thought is high time to work for union. So an attempt for union was initiated by A.C.Samuel, K.Kunjummen, and K.E.Abraham during their Missionary tour to United States in 1948. After much discussion at the headquarters of Assemblies of God in Missouri, plan of union was drawn and the Assemblies of God leaders were happy for the union. But due to the unwillingness of Assemblies of God missionaries then working in Kerala the union was not taken place.[21] We do not find any attempt of union initiated by the leaders of the Pentecostal Church after the event. But youths and many laymen attempted for union and formed many inter-denominational forums for it. Pentecostal Youths belonging to all Pentecostal denomination joined together to organize 'All Kerala Pentecostal Youth Conference' at Thrikkanamangal Kottarakkara from 17th to 19th May, 1961. Church leaders such as T.M.Varghese, P.D.Johnson, P.M.Philip and P.J.Thomas representing Church of God, Assemblies of God, IPC and Sharon Fellowship spoke in the different sessions of the conference.[22] This was the first attempt initiated by the youth which was fully supported by the leaders of the church. The next meeting of such initiated by the youth was held after a long period of eighteen years in 1980 at Puthupally, Kottayam. This conference has passed a resolution requesting the church leaders to work out for the union of all Pentecostal churches in Kerala.[23] A Pentecostal weekly began to publish in 1978 by the name "Good News" stimulated the union effort by publishing news and views of all denominations. Through the powerful writings of V.M.Mathew (Chairman), C.V.Mathew (Editor) and other editorial board members

---

[21] K.E.Abraham, *Yesukristhuvinte....*, p.382.

[22] "All Kerala Pentecostal Youth Conference", *Assemblies of God Messenger*, 7/10, (June, 1961): pp.21, 22.

[23] "Samyuktha Yuvajana Camp – 1980 Passakkiya Premeyam" (Malayalam) [A resolution passed by Youth Camp held in 1980], Good news, 3/18 (April 10, 1980): p.1.

convinced the readers about the urgent need for unity and could bring all the Pentecostal leaders together in connection with the anniversary of "Good News" in February 1979.[24] Then onwards many united conventions and camp meetings were held and at present there is a trend among the Pentecostals for union.

There are many inter-denominational forums, and organizations such as Association of Pentecostal Theological Institutions (APTI-May 1979), Inter Collegiate Prayer Fellowship (ICPF-October 1982), Pentecostal Press Association (PPA-1985), Christian Revival Movement (CRM-1987), Kerala Pentecostal Fellowship (KPF-1989)[25] etc. From 1979 onwards a number of interdenominational organizations were formed, and it shows the desire for unity. These interdenominational organizations helped much in the co-operation between different Pentecostal denominations in Kerala. United conventions were held at Tiruvalla, Kottayam and Ranny in 1990, 1992 and 1994. Though most of these union efforts were initiated by lay leaders, it became an eye-opener to the leaders of the church and began to support those movements. Thus in 1990's we find more co-operations among the different denominations.

4.4. Indian Identity

Since the Pentecostal movement began in Kerala as a missionary enterprise, Pentecostalism is understood as a new sect imported from the West, especially from the United States of America. The foreign missionaries, who always like to continue the work in the third world countries as an extension of the work in the homeland, did not attempt to develop the churches in India as Indian Church, but as American and European churches. The missionaries who controlled and

---

[24] "Goodnews Anniversary", Goodnews, 2/7 (February, 1979), pp.1-3.

[25] K.J.Mathew, *op.cit.,* pp.115-121.

supervised the work in Travancore provided financial assistance for the work. The natives who received financial support from the missionary societies were considered as the agents of missionaries who caused an antipathy towards them in the community. About it K.E.Abraham says: "People blame the ministry as the ministry of money because they receive financial assistance from the missionaries."[26] The native leaders understood that too much dependence on the missionary societies would make the Pentecostals to remain as a potted plant alienated from the general soil of the Indian society. Therefore to develop an identity of its own the native leadership took an independent step. It was impossible for the natives to take a decision by themselves as far as they depend on foreign mission body. Foreigners always tried to maintain their master attitude and natives were dissatisfied in their attitude.

Therefore the natives argued to register the land in the name of local church in 1925. Though the missionaries disagreed at first natives took strong step and the property bought for the churches were registered in the name of local church. Then onwards we find different steps taken by the natives helped the Pentecostal churches to develop an identity of their own. After transferring the leadership responsibilities to the natives, Assemblies of God also decided to register the property to the respective districts in 1973.[27]

Under the native leadership men of talent, quality and vision were drawn to the ministry and there was a general feeling among the members that the church belongs to them and there is something they themselves must do. Thus when the native leadership was emerged among the Pentecostals in Kerala, there developed an identity of their own, which is different from the western culture.

---

[26] K.E.Abraham, "Suvisesha Parisramam....", p.68.
[27] Benjamin Prasad Shinde, *op.cit.*, p.183.

4.5. Theological Education

One of the major hindrances usually put forward for the development of indigenous leadership is the lack of educated people available among the natives as their western friends. At first, there was no systematic theological education provided to the ministers. But the people from Syrian Christian community, who had some knowledge in the scripture and have potential leadership were used to propagate the Pentecostal teaching. Though George Berg the first Pentecostal missionary expressed 'the need for two Bible schools, one at Nilgiri and other at Travancore, for the training of natives, they could establish the first Bible School only in 1926 at Mavelikkara. Cook and K.E.Abraham started Bible Schools at Mulakkuzha in 1928 and Kumbanad in 1930. All these schools meant for training the natives for the evangelization of the unreached areas.

At the beginning, academic performance was not given much importance but when the number of institutions increased serious attempts was made to develop the standard of the schools to improve the academic excellence. Institutions began to offer theological degrees, both English and Malayalam are used as the medium of instruction. Though there was antipathy towards theological education under Serampore system, it was changed by 1980's and Pentecostal seeks theological education in the graduate, post-graduate and doctoral level under the recognized university system. An interdenominational organization known as Pentecostal Society for Theological Studies (PSTS) formed in 1992 to promote theological education on post-graduate and doctoral level among the Pentecostals.[28] At present church gives importance for the theological training and each denominations has their own institutions. Those who had a proper theological training were only appointed as pastors of the church.

---

[28] Brochure, Pentecostal Society for Theological Studies, Tiruvalla, 1992, pp.1-2.

4.6.   Missionary Work

The missionaries came to Kerala for the propagation of the Pentecostal teachings, and in the early period the Pentecostal work was mainly depended on the missionaries sent from abroad. The situation changed by the middle of the century. The institutions established to train the natives produced many trained ministers and moved to the different parts of Kerala and even sent to the other states in India. Many natives had been sent to different parts of the country and they established many churches. Indian Evangelical Team organized by P.G.Varghese, Peniel Gospel team by Joseph Mammen, Christian Fellowship by Kurian Thomas are some of the work mainly concentrated in North India.[29] Indian Pentecostal Church also formed a Mission Board in 1969 to support financially the work outside Kerala[30] and offering of the 2nd Sunday of September is set apart for it. In 1994, Assemblies of God Church formed a mission board and it send its seven missionaries to North India, and these missionaries are financially supported by the Malayalam District of AG.[31] The Sharon Fellowship Church has 231 churches outside Kerala, and the missionary training centers were started in Andhra Pradesh, Gujarat and New Delhi to train the natives for missionary work.[32] Thus under native leadership churches in Kerala have improved from receiving missionaries to send missionaries to other states.

---

[29] Saju, *Kerala Pentecosthu Charithram*, p.188.

[30] T.G.Oommen, IPC yum..... p.40.

[31] Finny George and K.J.Mathew, "Kristiya Sabhacharithram Oru Padanam Noottandukalilude" (Malayalam) [A Study on history of Christianity through the centuries], Punalur: SIAG Malayalam District Council, 1996, pp.125-126.

[32] Cherian Mathew (ed.), Darshanam, 1996-97 a Magazine From Faith Theological Seminary, Manakala: FTS, 1997, p.8.

Conclusion

The State of Kerala, where more Christians are found in South India, enjoyed the fruits of three great revivals occurred during the latter part of the 19th century and the beginning of the 20th century, became a prepared field for the Pentecostal missionaries, who set out to propagate the teachings, following the great revivals in United States. India was under British rule and as a result of rising nationalism, Indians desired for the independence and they began to fight for it. Besides, western education which is based on reason and judgment urged the elite of India to shed its rigidity of thought and assimilate the critical and creative thought of the West. In the age of enlightenment they thought it is better to be self-reliant.

Since the missionaries identified themselves with the ruling class, natives considered them as the agents of British government. When the struggle for Indian independence was so acute, the Indian church also began to think seriously about the independence of the Church from the missionary control. Reformed group separated from Jacobite Church and established Mar Thoma Syrian Church under the native leadership. Later Orthodox Syrian Church constituted the seat of Catholics in 1912, also became independent from Antiochean Patriarchate. There were also attempts among the protestant circles, to achieve the native leadership, since 1850's. Pentecostals too inherit the same background, began to strive for the independence of the Church from the missionary control. Thus there were struggles between native leaders and missionaries. The missionaries, who direct and finance the mission work, did not like to hand over the responsibilities to the natives at first. Missionary was considered as the paymaster of the Indian mission workers and it is not always easy for him to come to a close contact with them.

In its struggle for indigenous leadership, Pentecostal churches have great achievement. In its early stage itself struggle for the indigenous leadership began and a group came under native leadership in 1930. Church under native leadership progressed in number and it challenged others to apply the same principle. The two World Wars interrupted the arrival of missionaries and in the wake of Indian Independence missionaries themselves made arrangements for transferring their responsibilities to the natives. Though most of the churches obtained indigenous leadership there are many other areas yet to progress which remain as challenges to the Indian leadership.

One of the most important challenges which Indian leadership faces is the financial dependence on foreign sources for the various activities of the church. India is a third world country and government as well as the christian and other faith organization depend on foreign money is the excuse put forward to justify the dependence. But there are people who question the dependence of natives on foreign mission agencies for financial support and challenge to overcome the dependence on foreign money. The steps taken for the self-support of the church became helpful to the growth of the church while the Swedish money received by Indian Pentecostal Church leaders caused the Full Gospel Church in Malabar, progressing independently under Cook, to come under the administrative control of Church of God, Cleveland, Tennesse. Dependence on foreign money became a stumbling block to the progress of indigenous church. It became harm rather, a help to the church in India. Thus the present challenge among the native leadership is to find out some source to meet the needs of Indian Church and make the church independent from foreign money.

The great problem which Pentecostals face today is disunity. Though the division helped to the progress of the church, it became a great abomination among the people. Even though attempts were made to unite all Pentecostal churches, unity is not yet completely achieved. There are many miles to be covered on the road to unity since all groups were working without much co-operation for a long time. It is not very easy to come to an organic union. Now the attempts were made mainly to work out unity in Mission and organic unity is not emphasized. Many laymen blame leadership of the Pentecostal churches as obstacle for unity and there is growing interest among the members to work out for unity. It also challenges the native leadership to work for the unity of the church.

Most of the people who followed the Pentecostal teaching were from poor and depressed class. Even from the very beginning Pentecostals provided help for the needy though not in an organized form. It was mainly taking into account of 'Jesus' words: "when you give to the needy, do not let your left hand know what your right hand is doing, so that your giving may be in secret" (Mathew 6.3,4-NIV). The Pentecostals give emphasize to the salvation of human soul rather than the physical body. Pentecostals have no institutions like hospitals, schools, colleges etc., and it is an area in which more attention should be given.

Bibliography

1. BOOKS

Abraham, K.E. *Yesukristhuvinte Eliya Dasan Athava Pastor K.E. Abraham* (Mal.) [Humble servant of Jesus Christ or Pastor K.E.Abraham] Autobiography, 2nd ed, Kumbanand: K.E.Abraham Foundation, 1983.

Abraham, K.E. *IPC Praramba Varshangal* (Mal.) [The early years of IPC], 2nd ed, Kumbanad: K.E.Abraham Foundations, 1986.

Abraham, T.P. *Naveekaranam – Thudakkavum Thudarchayum* (Mal.) [Revival – beginning and continuation], Kottayam: The Ashram Press, 1985.

Abraham, T.S. *Pentacosthu Prasthanam* (Mal.) [Pentecostal Movement], Kumbanad: Hebron Book Depot, 1969.

Adhav, Shamsunder Manohar. *Pandita Ramabai,* Madras: CLS, 1979.

Agur, C.M. *Church History of Travancore,* New Delhi: Asian Educational Service, 1990.

Aprem, Mar and T.P. Abraham eds. *Sabha Charitra Nighandu* (Mal.) (Dictionary of Church History), Tiruvalla: TLC, 1986.

Aprem, Mar. *Indian Christian Directory,* Bangalore: Bangalore Parish of the Church of the East, 1984.

Ayroor, Daniel. *Keralathila Pentecosthu Sabhakal* (Pentecostal Churches in Kerala), Mavelikkara: Beer Sheba Bible College, 1986.

Azariah, V.S. *India and Missions,* London: CLS, 1909.

Bernard, K.L.*Flashes of Kerala History,* Cochin: K.L.Bernard, 1977.

Bresson, Bernard. *Studies in Ecstacy,* New York: Vantage Press, 1966.

Browne, Michael. *Autonomy and Authority.* Scotland: Gospel Treact Publications, 1988.

Buregess, Stanley M. and Gary B. McGee. eds. *Dictionary of Pentecostal and Charismatic Movements,* Michigan: Zondervan Publishing House, 1990.

Carothers, W.F. *The Baptism with the Holy Ghost Speaking in Tongues,* Illionois: Carothers, 1907.

Chacko, E.J. *Keralathile Chila Swathanthra Sabhakal* (Mal.) [some of the independent churches in Kerala], Thiruvalla: TLC, 1986.

Cherian, C.V. *Indian History, Vol.II,* Trivandrum: Kerala University Central Co-operative Storels Ltd., 1991.

Cook, Robert F.*A Quarter Century of Divine Leading in India,* Chengannur: Church of God in India, 1939.

__________*Half a century of Divine Leading and 37 Years of Apostolic Achievements in South India,* Tennesse: Church of God Foreign Mission Department, 1955.

Conn, Charles W. *Like a Mighty Army,* Tennesse: Church of God Publishing House, 1955.

Daniel, Mathew. Sadhu Kochukunjupadesi (Mal.) [a short biography of Sadhu Kochukunja], Tiruvalla: CLS, 1988.

Davies, Horton. *The Challenge of The Sects,* London: SCM Press, 1963.

Dupre, Louis and Don E.Salires, eds. *World Spirituality, An* Encyclopeadic History of the Religious Quest, Vol III: Christian Spirituality Post Reformation and Modern, *New York:* The Crossroad Publishing Company, 1991.

Durasoff, Steve. *Bright Wind of the Spirit: Pentecostalism Today,* New Jersey Logos International, 1972.

Dyer, Helen S. *Revival in India,* London: Margon & Scott, 1907.

Eapen, K.V. *Church Missionary Society and Education in Kerala,* Kottayam: Kollett Publications 1985.

______________,*History of the Church Missionary Society in Kerala,* Kottayam: Kollettu Publication, 1985.

______________,*A Study of Kerala History,* Kottayam: Kollett Publications, 1971.

Easow, T.E. *Brethren Presthanam Lokamengum* (Mal.). [Brethrens all over the world], Koratty. (Kerala):Universal Press, 1981.

Eddy, Sherwood. *India Awakening,* New York: Missionary Education Movement, 1911.

Elanthoor, Achenkunja, *Pentecosthukarodu Mathram,* (Mal.). [only to the Pentecostals], Tiruvalla: Deepthi Books, 1991.

______________,ed. *Unarvinte Jwalakal* (Mal.) [flames of revival]. Kottayam: PPAI, 1992.

Fey, Harold E, *A History of the Ecumenical Movement, Vol. II,* 1948-1968 2nd ed., Geneva: WCC,1986.

Firth, C.B. *An Introduction to Indian Church History,* Madras: CLS, 1983.

George, Finny and K.J.Mathew. *Kristhiya Sabhacharithram Oru Padanam Noottandukaliloode* (Mal.) [A study of the History of Christianity through the centuries], Punalur: SIAG Malayalam District Council, 1996.

Gibbs, M.E. *From Jerusalem to New Delhi: the Story of the Christian Church,* Madras: CLS, 1978.

______________,*The Anglican Church in India 1600-1970,* New Delhi: ISPCK, 1972.

Gladstone, J.W. *Protestant Christianity and People's Movement in Kerala 1850-1936,* Trivandrum: Seminary Publications, 1984.

Halburt, Jessy Leeman. *Kristhu Sabha Charithram* (mal) [history of the Christian Church], Punaloor: Malayalam District of SIAG, 1954.

Hodges, Melvin L. *The Indigenous Church,* Springfield: Gospel Publishing House, 1971.

Hoell, Nills Bloch. *The Pentecostal Movement: It's Origin, Development and Distinctive Character,* London: George Allen & Unwin Ltd., 1964.

Hollenweger, Walter J. *The Pentecostals,* London: SCM Press Ltd, 1972.

Hollis, Michael. *Paternalism and the Church A study of South Indian Church History,* London: Oxford University Press, 1962.

Hunt, W.S., *The Anglican Church in Travancore and Cochin* 1816-1916 Operations of the Church Missionary Society *in South West India,* Kottayam: Church Missionary Society, 1920.

Jacob, John A. *A History of the London Missionary Society in South Travancore,* 1806-1959, Nagarcoil: Diocean Press, 1990.

Johnson, P.D. *Vagdatha Nivarthi* (Mal.) [Promise Fulfilled] Trivandrum: P.D.Johnson, 1968.

Joy, K.T. *The Mar Thoma Church: A Study of Its Growth and Contribution,* Kottayam: K.T.Joy, 1983.

Keay, F.E. *A History of the Syrian Church in India,* Delhi: ISPCK, 1960.

Koshy, M.J. *Last Days of Monarchy in Kerala,* Trivandrum: Kerala Historical Society, 1973.

Kuriakose, M.K. *History of Christianity in India: Source Materials,* Madras: CLS, 1982.

Korean, T.A. Maharani K.V.Simon (Mal.) [Biography of K.V. Simon], Angamali: Premier Printers, 1990.

Kuruvilla, K.K. *Keralathile Almiya Unarvu* (Mal.) [Spiritual Revival in Kerala], Thiruvalla: Malayalam Christian Literature Committee, 1942.

__________,*Bharathathile Kraisthava Sabhakal Oru Samshipta Charithram* (Mal.) [A brief history of Christian Churches in India], Thiruvalla: CLS, n.d.

__________, *A History of Mar Thoma Church and its Doctrines*, Madras: CLS, 1951.

Lopez, Lawrence. *A Social History of Modern Kerala*, Trivandrum: Lawrence Lopez, 1988.

McDearmid, Andrew 'The Pentecostal Churches of India' in George Mennacheri (ed.) *The St.Thomas Christian Encyclopaedia of India Vol. I* Trichur: St.Thomas. Christian Encyclopaedia, 1982.

McGee, Gary B. *Selected Documents on the History of the Assemblies of God in India*, Spring field: Assemblies of

God, 1991.

Menon, A.Sreedhara. *A Survey of Kerala History* Kottayam: Sahitya Pravarthaka Co-Operative Society Ltd., 1970.

Menzies, William W. *Antointed to Serve: A Story of the Assemblies of God*, Missouri: Gospel Publishing House, 1971.

Moon, Elmer Louis. *The Pentecostal Church: A History of Popular Survey*, New York: Carlton Press, 1966.

Mundadan, A. Mathias. *Indian Christian's search for Identity and Struggle for Autonomy*, Bangalore: Dharmaram Publications, 1984.

Myers, Dora P. *Daivasabha Charithram* (Mal.) [Church of God History], Mulakkuzha: CGI Press, 1960.

Neill, Stephen. et al., eds. *Concise Dictionary of the Christian World Mission*, London: Lultworth Press, 1970.

Neill, Stephen, *The Story of the Christian Church in India and Pakistan*, Madras: CLS-ISPCK, 1972.

Newton, K.J. *Glimpses of Indian Church History*, India: Living Light Publications, 1975.

Oommen T.G. *Atmakatha* (Mal.) [Auto-biography], Kuwait: Kuwait IPC, 1984.

__________,*IPC Yum Anpathu Varshathe Sevana Charithravum* (Mal.) [IPC and its fifty years service], Mallappally: Mallappally Printers, 1979.

Orr, J.Edwin. *Evangelical Awakenings in India in the Early Twentieth Century*, New Delhi: Masih Sahitya Sansth, 1970.

Philip, Mammen. *Robert F.Cook (Mal.)*, vennikkulam: Deepam book club, 1992.

Philip, T.V. *Ecumenism in Asia*. Thiruvalla: CSS-ISPCK, 1994.

______________,'Protestant Christianity in India Since 1858', George Menacherri (ed.) *The St.Thomas Christian Encyclopaedia of India* Vol. I, Trichur: St.Thomas Encyclopedia of India, 1982.

Pospisil, William *Scriptural Church Government*, Mulakuzha: CGI Press, 1960.

Rao, M.Girinath. *Indian National Movement and Constitutional Development*. Guntur: Sidhartha Printers, 1985.

Saju, *Daivathinte Manushyan* (Mal.) [Man of God], Kurianoor: Margam Books, 1989.

______________, Kerala Penthekosthu Charithram (Mala.) [History of Kerala Pentecostals]. Kottayam: Goodnews Publications, 1994.

______________, *Nallavanum Visuvasthanumaya Dasan.* (Mal.) [Good and Faithful servant], Kottayam: Goodnews Publications, 1995.

Sam, L. *Pastor A.C.Samuel* (Mal.), Trivandrum: T.J.Rajan, 1983.

Samuel, A.C. *Assemblies of God* (Mal.). Trivandrum: SIAG Malayalam District, 1954.

Samuel, M.T. *Pentecosthu Presthanam Innale, Inne* (Mal.) [Pentecostal Movement yesterday, today], Kottayam: Goodnews Publications, 1988.

Samuel, Sunny P. *Pastor ART Athisayam, Unarvinte Theenalam* (ART Athisayam, flame of revival), Mulakkuzha: Bethestha Books, 1995.

Schafer, Heinrich. *Church Indentity Between Repression and Liberation: The Presbyterian Church in Guatemala.* (Trans. by Craig Koslofky) Geneeva: World Alliance of Reformed Churches, 1991.

Schoonmaker, Christian. *A Man who loved the will of God,* Missouri: AG Foreign Mission Department, 1959.

Simon, K.V. *Malankarayile Verpadu Sabhakalude Charithram.* (Mal.), [The History of the Brethrens Churches in Kerala], Kottayam: Chriasthavasramam Press, 1936.

Synan, Vinson ed. *Aspects of Pentecostal Charismatic Orgins,* New Jersy: Logos International, 1975.

Synan, Vinson. *The Holiness Pentecostal Movement in United States,* Grand Rapids: Eerdmans publishing company, 1971.

Tharappan, C.V. Kristhiya Sabha Charithram (Mal.) [History of Christian Church], 2nd ed, Kunnamkulam: K.O.Cheru, 1976.

Thoma, Juhanon Mar. *Christianity in India and a Brief History of the Mar Thoma Syrian Church.* Madras: K.M.Cherian, 1968.

Thomas, M.A. *An outline History of Christian Churches and Denominations in Kerala,* Trivandrum: M.A. Thomas, 1977.

Thomas, M.M. and P.T. Thomas. *Towards an Indian Christian Theology,* Thiruvalla: New Day Publications, 1992.

Thomas, M.M. Abraham Malpante Naveekarnam Oru Vyakyanam (Mal.) [An Interpretation of Revival by Abraham Malpan], Tiruvalla: TLC, 1984.

Tippett, Alan R. *Verdict Theology in Missionary Anthropology,* South Pasadena: William Carey Library, 1973.

Varghese, Titus V. & P.P. Philip. *Glimpses of the History of the Christian Churches in India,* Madras: CLS, 1983.

Varghese, Habel G. *K.E.Abraham. An Apostle from Modern India,* Kadambanad: The Christian Literature service of India, 1974.

Varghese, T.M. & E.V. George. *Anpathu Varshangal* (Mal.) [Fifty Years], Mulakuzha: Church of God Literature service, 1973.

Vadakel, Sebestian. *An Indigenous Missionary Endeavour,* Vadavathoor: Oriental Institute of Religion Studies India, 1990.

Pastor Paul: Jeevacharithra Samgraham (Mal) [a short biography of Pastor Paul.], Trivandrum: Pentecostal Press Trust, 1994.

2. PERIODICALS

Abraham, K.E. "Indian Pentecosthu Swathantra Sabhakal (Mal.) [Independent Pentecostal Churches in India], *Zion Kahalam* 2/7 (July, 1938).

_______________,Jnangalude Naveena Padhathi (Mal.) [Our new plan], *Suvesha prabhashakan* 2/12 (July, 1929).

_______________, "Sthalam Subhakalude Swathanthriam" (Mal.) [Independence of the local church] *Zion Kahalam* 11/5 (May, 1952).

Abraham, K.E. "Suvisesha Parisramam Indiayil Vijayapradhama-kunnathe Enganne?" (Mal.) [how can the evangelization in India be victorious], *Zion Kahalam* 2/2 & 3 (February-March, 1938).

Abraham, T.P. "Puthiya Presthanangal Einiyum Avasyamo?" (Mal) [is there any need of new organizations], *Swargeeya Dwani* (May, 1996).

Abraham, T.S. "Kumbanadu Convention Innarambikkunnu" (Mal) [Kumbanadu convention begins today] *Malayala Manorama,* Kottayam: (January 12, 1997).

Abrams, Minnie F. "How Pentecost Came to India?", The *Pentacostal Evangel* (May, 1945)

Bhaskaran, N.K. "The Ezhava Memorial and the Founding of SNDP Yogam", *Journal of Kerala Studies,* Vol.IX, (December, 1982).

"Thousands Eager for the Gospel" *The Latter Rain Evangel.* (May, 1912).

Berg, George E. "Light and Shadows in India"*Latter Rain Evangel,* (September, 1912).

Burgess, John H. "Bible School Proves Blessing" *Pentecostal Evangal.* (March 18, 1935).

Chapman, Mary W. "Testimony" (Mal.),*Pentecosthu Kahalam,* 1/1, (November, 1925).

Cherian, K.C. "Sthalam Sabhakalude Swathanthriam" (Mal.) [Independence of the local Churches], *Zion Kahalam* 1/11, (November, 1937), Vol.1, No. 12, (December, 1937).Cook, R.F. "Alochana Sabha" (Council), *Suvisesha Prabhaahakan,3/4* (November, 1929).

Cook, Robert F. "Alochana Sabha" (Mal.) [Council], *Suvisesha Prabhashakan 3/4* (November, 1929).

______________ ,"Death of Sister Cook", *Weekly Evangel,* (November, 1917).

______________,"Pathradipa Lekhanam (Mal.) [editorial], *Suvisesha Prabhashakan, 3/8,* (March, 1930).

______________,"Sabhakariyam" (Mal.) [Church Matters], *Suvisesha Prabhashakan, 3/1 & 2*(August-September, 1929).

DuPlessis, David J. "The Historic Background of Pentecostalism", *One in Christ,* Vol.X (1974).

George, Babu. "Einium Presthanangal Untakatta" (Mal.) [Let there be more organizations], *Swargeeya Dwani,* (July, 1992).

George, T.C. "Pentacostal Church Growth in South India", *India Church Growth Quarterly,* 3/1 (January-March, 1981).

Graves, Carl.F. "Encouraging News from South India", *Pentecostal Evangel,* (February, 1933).

Hollenweger, Walter J. "After Twenty Years Research on Pente-costalism", *International Review of Mission,* 25/297 (January, 1986).

Jeyraj, Yesuadian. "From the Chairman". *The General Council of the Assemblies of God of India Bullettin,* (February, 1995).

Johnson, P.D. "K.E.Abraham Mahathvathil" (Mal.) [K.E.Abraham in glory], *Assemblies of God Messenger,* 22/3 (December, 1974).

Ketcham, M.L. "Churches in Progress", *Pentecostal Evangel* (February 5, 1983)

______________,"Travancore", *The Missionary Challenge* (January, 1954).

Kucera, Martha M. "Report" *Pentecostal Evangel* (August 19, 1933) & (November, 1934).

Mammen, V.P. "Nammude Sabhayile Unarve" (Mal.) [Revival of Our Church], *Malankara Sabha Tharaka,* 4/5 (October, 1907).

Mathai, Varghese. "Hebron Bible Collegil Classukal Aarambichu" (Mal.) [Classes began in Herbron Bible College], *Malabar Gospel Messenger,* 6/20, (May 20, 1996).

Mathew, John. "Pastor T.M.Varghese" (Mal.) *Suvisesha Dwani,* 22/10 (October, 1972).

______________,"Pastor C.G.Varghese" (Mal.) *Suvisesha Dwani,* 22/11 (November, 1972).

McGee, Gary B. "The Azusa Street Revival and Twentieth Century Missions", *International Bullettin of Missionary Research,* (April, 1988).

Monai, C.P. "Thomachayanum Valarunna Sharonum" (Mal.) [P.J.Thomas and Growing Sharon], *Subavani* (November, 1992).

Nelson, Reed E. "Five Principles of Indigenous Church Organization: Lesson from a Brazilian Pentecostal Church", *Missiology: An International Review,* 17/1 (January, 1989).

Pethrus, Levi. "Indians Brothers" (Mal.), *Zion Kahalam Yathavasara Lekha,* No.4 (April, 1937).

Perumpetty, Vijoy Scariah. "Charithravarthanampol Kanniyatra Swaninte Nattilekke" (First tour to the country of Swan as a repetition of history) in *Malabar*

Gospel Messenger (Mal.), 10/42 (October, 1996).

Philip, K.P. "Parisudhalama Snana Sakshiyangel" (Mal.) [Testimony of the baptism in the Holy Spirit], *Suvisesha Prabhashakan*, 3/ 1 & 2(August-September, 1929).

Philip, P.S. "Puthuvarshathilekk Pratheekshakalude" (Mal.) [With expections to the new year], (January, 1994).

Saju, "Keralathile Pentecostu Sabhakalude Aarambavum Valarchayum"

(Mal.) [origin and growth of Pentecostal churches in Kerala], *Goodnews*, 16/10 (March, 1993).

Samuel, P.M. "Parisudhalma Snana Sakshiam" (Mal.) [Testimony of the baptism in the Holy Spirit], *Suvisesha Prabhashakan*, 3/3(October, 1929).

Samuel, Sabu. "Hebron Bible College" (Mal.) *Malabar Gospel Messenger*, 5/16, (April 16, 1995).

Sepulveda, Juan. "Pentecostalism as Popular Religiosity" *International Review of Mission*, 28/11, (January, 1989).

Stephen, M., "The Challenge of the Pentecostal Churches Today: A Insiders View", *Jeevadhara*, 25/148, (July, 1995).

Stubbs, C.Earl. "Golden Jubilee", *Pentecostal Witness* (March, 1997).

Sugeetha, G. "The Constitutional Progress in Travancore in the 19th and 20th Centuries", *Journal of Kerala studies*, Vol.VIII (December, 1981).

Thomas, P.B. "Pentecostal Ecclesiology: Promises and Problems", *Jeevadhara*, Vol.XX (1990).

Thomas, Shibu. "Assemblies of God General Convention" (Mal.), *Swargeeya Dwani*, (February, 1991).

Varghese, T.M. "A Forward Move" (Mal.), *Suvisesha Prabhashakan*, 3/9 & 10 (April- May, 1930).

Varghese, T.M. "Parisudhalma Snana Sakshiangal" (Mal.) [testimony of the baptism in the Holy Spirit], 3/1 & 2 (August-September, 1929).

Yohannan, Finny.C. "Suvisesha Poralikalude Janma Grihathilekk" (Mal.) [to the birthplace of Gospel warriers], *Edayanta Sabdam,* 13/2 (June-July, 1996).

"All Kerala Pentecostal Youth Conference" (Mal.), *Assemblies of God Messenger,* 7/10 (June, 1961).

"Assemblies of God Convention" (Mal.) *Hallelujah* (January, 1997).

"Assemblies of God Convention Ee Azhchayil" (Mal.) [Assemblies of God convention in this week], *Hallelujah,* 2/2 (February 15, 1996).

"Bible School" (Mal.) *Suvisesha Prabhashakan,* 2/10 & 11, 11(May-June, 1929).

"Editorial" (Mal.), *Malankara Sabha Tharaka* [star of Malabar church], 4/4, (September, 1907).

"Goodnews Anniversary" (Mal.), *Goodnews,* 2/7 (February, 1979).

"Hebron Bible School." (Mal.) *Zion Kahalam,* 2/8 (August, 1938).

"India Daivasabha Kerala State Convention" (Mal.) *Goodnews* (February 6, 1985).

"Pathradhipa Kurippukal" (Mal.) [Editorial notes], *Malankara Sabha Tharaka,* 4/5 (October, 1907).

"Report", *Pentecostal Evangel* (August, 1926).

"Report", *Pentecostal Evangel* (July 6, 1929).

"Report" (Mal.), *Pentecosthu Kahalam,* 1/2 (November, 1925).

"Samyukta Yuvajana Camp- 1980 Passakkiya Premeyam" (Mal.) [resolution passed by the United Youth Camp -1980] *Goodnews,* 3/18 (April 10, 1980).

"The Late Missionary Mrs.Mary Chapman" (Mal.), *Pentecosthu Kahalam,* 3/2 (December, 1927).

"Thekkan Thiruvithamkur Convention" (Mal.) [convention in South Travancore] *Suvisesha Prabhashakan,* 2/8 & 9 (October, 1929).

"Two Indian Minister's Visit to England" (Mal.) *Zion Kahalam,* 2/1 (January, 1938).

3. BROCHURES AND SOUVENIRS

"Faith Promise", *Brochure,* Adoor: FTS, 1996.

"Pentecostal Society for Theological Studies" *Brochure,* Tiruvalla: PSTS, 1992.

Bethel Bible School Golden Jubilee Souvenir, Punalur: Bethel Bible School, 1977.

Christian Evangelical Movement Silver Jubilee Souvenir 1957-1982, Tiruvalla: CEM, 1982.

Church of God in India Kerala State General Convention Souvenir, Mulakkuzha: State council of CGI, 1996.

Church of God (Full Gospel) in India, Thuvayoor, Platinum Jubilee Souvenir, Thuvayoor: Church 1987.

Faith Theological Seminary College Magazines, Adur: FTS, 1990,'91'97.

Faith Theological Seminary Silver Jubilee Souvenir, Adur: FTS, 1995.

Salem Tract Society Silver Jubilee Souvenir, Vakathanam: Salem Tract Society, 1985.

The IPC Jubilee Souvenir (1924-1974) Kumbanad: Hebron Printing Press, 1974.

4. REPORTS AND UNPUBLISHED BOOKS

Holleman, Carl D. *South India,* (June, 1978)

Ketcham, M.L. *India-History of Pentecost,* Springfield, (n.d.)

Maloney, C.T. *Missionary Conference Report on South India and Ceylon,* held at Springfield, Missouri from March 16-18, 1943.

Mathew, K.J. *Denominational Pluralism among the Pentecostals in Kerala: Causes and Responses, 1920 to the Present.* M.Th.Thesis, Senate of Serampore College, 1993.

Mathew, Samuel. *The Pentecostal Churches in Kerala and its witness in the Socio-political life,* M.Th.Thesis, Senate of Serampore College, 1990.

Samuel, T.J. *The origin and Development of Assemblies of God in Kerala,* Report Presented in All-India General Conference of AG held in Delhi in February, 1995.

Shinde, Benjamin Prasad, *The Contribution of the Assemblies of God to Church Growth in India,* M.A.Thesis, Fuller Theological Seminary, 1974.

Scariah, Mathew P. *"An Evaluation of the History of the Assemblies of God Church in Kerala and Proposals for the Unity among the Pentecostal Churches in Kerala",* M.Th.Thesis, Senate of Serampore College, 1996.

Thomas, George. *Christian Indians and Indian Nationalism 1885-1950 An Interpretation in Historical and Theological Perspective* D.Th.dissertation, University of Hamburg, 1979.

5. OFFICIAL DOCUMENTS

The Constitution And By-Laws of the South India Assemblies of God, Punalur: The Planters Printing and Publishing house, 1957

Directory of Missionaries to India Holding Certificates of Appointment from the Assemblies of God, Springfield, 1922

Memmorandum of Sharon Fellowship Church, (1975).

Revised Constitution of Indian Pentecostal Church of God, Kumbanad: 1979.

Supplement to the General Assembly Minutes and Church of God [Full Gospel] in India Policy. Mulakkuzha: CGI Press, 1976.

6. CORRESPONDENCES

Letter addressed to Benjamin Prasad Shinde, Tejewadi, Junnar, Poona. From Miss.Mildred Ginn, Dated 28th February, 1974.

Letter addressed to Dr.Gary B.McGee, AG Theological Seminary, Springfield, from George and Mariam Cook dated 19th September 1985.

Letter addressed to the IPC Ministers, Kumbanad, from K.E.Abraham (Mal.), dated 9th August 1937.

Letter addressed to P.T.Mathew, Podimala, Poowathoor, from A.R.Thankayya Athisayam, (Mal.) dated 14th May 1929.

7. PERSONAL INTERVIEWS

Interview with Pastor K.V.Daniel at his residence (Trichur) on 12th December 1996.

Interview with Pastor E.V.George, at his residence, (Edamon, Punalur) on 12th November 1996.

Interview with Pastor K.M.Joseph at his residence (Vadavathoor) on 15th January, 1997.

Interview with Pastor E.Mammachan, at his residence (Urikunnu) on 12th November, 1996.

Interview with Pastor P.M.Philip, at his residence (Vadavathoor, Kottayam), on 11th January, 1997.

Interview with Pastor T.J.Samuel, at his residence (Karavaloor, Punalur) on 12th November, 1996.

Interview with Pastor P.J.Thomas, at his residence (Tiruvalla) on 29th January, 1997.